Mess on the Mara

A Friends-to-Lovers Romance

Cher Terais

Aggrandis Group, LLC

Also by Cher Terais

♥

A Wanderlust Romance

Bali Blue

Tempest in Tulum

Stay even more connected by scanning the the QR Code

below to access the fun stuff:

The soundtrack to this book and the others;

Inspiration boards and visuals for each book;

Free downloadables, short stories and more!

https://linktr.ee/Cher_Terais

The trip doesn't stop here! The Booked Club community and podcast

are COMING SOON!

Sign up for my mailing list for all the deets: https://bit.ly/cherter

aismailinglist

Mess on the Mara

A Friends-to-Lovers Romance

Cher Terais

Aggrandis Group, LLC

www.cherterais.com

ISBN: 978-1-7378260-4-0

Acknowledgements

♥

I've gotta tell you, thanking people was a piece of cake when I penned my first novel, Bali Blue. Back then, I was about as clueless as a chameleon in a bag of Skittles, and my list of helpers was as short as a hiccup.

But, as the old saying goes, when you know better, you do better. Or perhaps it's when you know what you don't know, your circle of victims – I mean, consultants – expands exponentially. For my second novel, Mess on the Mara, I had questions galore and a host of sweet folks to help answer them. So, sit tight as I show my gratitude to the brave souls who survived my incessant inquiries:

To my fearless travel buddy and brother, Muhammed McIntee-Masud: Thanks for braving Kenya with me. Without you as my tour guide, I wouldn't have dared to board a crop duster on a dirt runway in the middle of the Maasai Mara. Really, who else would join me in doing something so unapologetically crazy?

To the savior of my literary journey, Mila Hunt, and the Brag Chat Authors Group: I swear, before joining this group and our one on one sessions, I had no idea about Book Funnel, Amazon Ads, and Mark Dawson. Who are these people? Now, not only am I writing better love stories, but I'm also mastering the business of being an author. Much gratitude for making me less clueless.

Nikko J. Cooper, you beautiful Florida man: That steamy final sex scene wouldn't be half as spicy without your X-rated insights. Your contribution to this novel was... unique, to say the least. Please keep writing. You have a story to tell and the world needs to hear your advice.

To my scribes-in-arms and accountability partners, authors Mila Hunt and J. Nicole: There aren't enough pages in this book to contain my gratitude for you. Also, to my stand-in copy editors Chevina Phillips and Andree Simmons, thanks for putting up with my chaos and coming through in the clutch on that first round of edits.

Andree Simmons and Asson Michel: Without your shoulders, my tears would have formed a pool deep enough to rival the Pacific. Thanks for sticking with me even when the writing got tough.

Last, but never least, my beloved Bali Blue ARC Team: You wonderful humans have become my personal cheer squad. Your unwavering encouragement is as potent as a double-shot espresso. Special shout out to Cheryl McGee, I took your feedback on

Kendrick's spicy talk to heart and revised them all :) – Girl they were a little corny. LOL

So, here's to all you "unlucky souls" (I say that with all the love in the world) who helped make this novel possible. Without you, I'd be a writer adrift, shouting at the Instagram and TikTok algorithms, and probably still stuck at an airport in Kenya.

For my devoted readers, those who believe in the extraordinary power of love, who celebrate black women and the tireless men who journey to the ends of the earth for them. Your unwavering dedication gives these stories life. Together, we delve into the layered narratives of love and the shadows of generational trauma. You are my beacon, and for that, I offer my deepest gratitude.

Prologue – Andra

♥

"**A**NDRA!" MY MOM YELLED from the bottom of the stairs. "Bring your ass, lil' girl, you can't miss the bus today. I have to go to the studio and can't be late! Got a new artist to meet with!"

My momma's yelling was nothing new. Her normal morning voice on a workday was a shout and typically stayed in a shout until either I did what she needed me to hurry up so she wouldn't be late for work. It was hilarious to me how she'd be hollering like a banshee with me, but would totally switch it up to prim, proper professional when the phone rang or at work. That was my mother eighty percent of the time, aloof, calm, collected art curator..

"I'm coming," I yelled back as I swiped on the bubble gum pink lip gloss and took a final look at my baggy jeans, mock crop top and matching pink and white Retro 1s, but it was the sound of the school bus coming over the hill that lit the fire under my butt.

"Oh, crap. I need to go." I said out loud. I grabbed my book bag and bounded down the steps two at a time. I planted a kiss on my mom's cheek as I passed her on the way out the door, making sure to miss her signature bright red lipstick.

I ran down the block towards the bus stop. A big U-Haul truck was parked on the curb blocking the sidewalk. *Jerks.* I almost got my shoes dirty, having to hop a puddle on the street, when I had to walk around the monstrous truck. I had Mr. Washington's class first block this morning and the folks moving into the big empty house at the corner of Wadley and Tiger Flowers Drive were about to make me mess up my fresh!

I walked into my 7th grade algebra class, perfectly timed to make a grand entrance. I always got there just before the late bell, making sure to bend over and dust off the imaginary dirt on my Jays. Drawing the exact attention I was looking for from the fellow sneaker heads in class and just before Mr. Washington closed the door. Nobody, including me, wanted to be on the wrong side of that door when it closed. Mr. Wash didn't play about tardiness to his class. May as well keep on moving to the office to get a tardy slip before he'd let you in.

I took my seat right in front of my teacher's desk, ready to discuss last night's homework assignment. It was a little hard but I liked the challenge. I bet no one else in class even attempted to complete it. *More shine for me.*

I pulled out my work and was geeked in anticipation of my favorite teacher's attention. He was so cool and actually talked to us, instead of down to his students. He got us. He got me. He made math so fun and I took extra care with my homework. The reward was more of Mr. Washington's attention. I was the teacher's pet.

When he said stuff like, "If you had paid attention yesterday during my lesson like Andra, you would have gotten a higher score on that quiz," it made me smile and I usually sat up straighter. Or when he'd say, "Andra, go ahead and take a nap, while everyone else takes these notes, because you got it the first time around," I'd put my head down but mainly to daydream about him. I bet he'd make the perfect daddy.

Everyone loved Mr. Wash. Unlike most teachers, he took a hands-on approach to teaching. He often related our math lessons to things us 7th graders cared about. For instance, how the gamers in the class could increase the amount of time they could play video games in a day if they understood how to control the variables; sleep, chores, and homework, that might eat up their time.

For me, he related fractions and variables to my passion for cooking. He'd helped me countless times how to use the algebraic concepts to scale my recipes. He was the first male teacher I had. He was also the first teacher that took an interest in my interests outside the classroom. Perhaps that's why I was stoked to share with him how last night's homework helped me tweak the recipe for the batch of cookies I'd planned to make tonight for the class.

But Mr. Washington wasn't standing at the board. Nor did he make the announcement that typically came for everyone to take out their homework. Instead, he sat at his desk with a sad look on his face. I wanted to blurt out, "Mr. Wash, what's wrong?" But I didn't. Just sat there looking confused like everyone else in the class.

When he finally stood, edging around to sit at the corner of his desk facing us, he clasped his hands on his thighs in front of him, taking a deep breath. Everyone was silent, looking around at each other trying to figure out what was going on.

"Class," he started, giving us the most pitiful smile I'd ever seen. "Today is my last day teaching at McCullom Charter School."

Wait what? Surely I must have heard him wrong. I missed a good bit of his next words, trying to figure out how I had misunderstood the part about this being his last day. I was so busy trying to recreate his sentence that he was way down the line of what he was trying to get across by the time I tuned back in.

"I am getting married," he smiled ruefully like a little boy, "I'll be moving to Seattle to be with my fiancée. She's there finishing up law school." He pressed his lips together, splaying his hands and hunching his shoulders awkwardly, signaling he was done.

I audibly gasped. I hadn't misheard him. He was leaving. And before I could stop them, big boulder sized tears threatened to spring from my eyes. A knot grew in my throat. I'm not sure how long I sat there tuned all the way out of what Mr. Washington was saying. Who was going to give me new ways to split up my recipes. What other teacher could possibly make me feel less alone. *No one.*

I wanted to scream for him to shut up. Tell him to go on and leave, then. We didn't care. But I did care. I was pissed. My heart was pounding in my chest, threatening to rip right through it. As soon as the bell rang, I sprang to my feet, grabbing my book bag but not caring that I left that stupid homework assignment fluttering to the floor as I made a mad dash out of his class.

Hot tears burned my eyes as I tried to rush past the throng of students milling in the hallway before their next class. Skirting some of them, I hurried on towards the bathroom, not looking up until I ran into a wall of students blocking the door to the ladies room. It was a circle of them. Some laughed and jeered at whatever was happening in the center. Others were shaking their heads and pointing.

Their oohs and aahs mixed with disgusted looks of those wanting whatever was happening to stop, caught my attention. I edged closer to see everyone was pointing at a scrawny kid who was scrambling to pick up the scattered contents of his book bag from the floor. I didn't recognize him. Must have been a new kid.

My anger was already at its peak because I couldn't get into the bathroom to check the tears that had left a wet stream on my face,, but it hit white hot when I pushed through the crowd, to see Charles Ansley push the skinniest boy I'd ever seen before back down again, as soon as he'd stood up. The new kid hit the floor with a thud, his book bag and all his belongings sliding to the far side of the crowd.

Charles yelling, "Get up you black, African-booty-scratcher," was all it took to send me flying at him so fast knocking that coward off of his feet. I blacked out and started wailing on him, kicking and screaming.

"Call him that again! I bet you won't, you bug-ugly bully!" I kept swinging until I felt someone yank be off of him by my book bag. Even while up in the air, I still kicked and screamed, trying to rip that shocked look off of Charles' face.

I locked eyes with the skinny, new kid. He gave me a nod of thanks. I gave him a quick grin before being dragged down the hall to the principal's office by my book bag.

The only reason that I didn't get suspended for fighting was because Mr. Washington told the principal that I was defending the new kid. Kobena, or something like that, was his name. Thank god it was Mr. Washington who broke up the fight. Because my mom was going to kill me if I had gotten suspended and she had to miss work to come up to the school.

What I didn't know until Mrs. Monroe, the principal, told me, was that Mr. Washington had asked on my behalf not to suspend me for fighting. He'd explained to her that he broke the news to his class that today was his last day and that I didn't take it too well.

After sitting me down in her office, the principal smiled at me sympathetically.

"Andra, I understand how hard it can be to lose a great teacher like Mr. Washington. It can actually be kind of scary. Like losing someone."

When I started crying again, she pulled me into a hug, shushing me calmly while promising everything was going to be okay. But how could it when it felt like my daddy was leaving me again. After my tears subsided, Ms. Monroe let me stay in her office for the rest of the school day.

On the bus, I sat there staring out the window. Sad. But no more tears. I still felt some kind of way about losing my favorite teacher. I was so deep in thought that I didn't notice the new boy trying to get my attention.

"May I *seet?*" he asked in the thickest but most interesting accent I'd ever heard..

I snapped back to the present and stammered, "Yeah. sure," pulling my things closer to make room for him on the seat.

"I'm Kobena. Everyone calls me Kobe though," When we got to our block, Kobe invited me in to meet his mother and I was too excited to do so, especially when I smelled the wonderfully weird aroma of something cooking in her kitchen. Turned out, Kobe, his older brother, Kenji, their mom, and dad were the new family that moved in on my street.

Chapter 1 – Andra

♥

I STARED INTO THE camera lens, heart racing with excitement, but also with a little dread. The news we were about to share with our followers was a game changer, but I wasn't sure if we were ready for what was to come.

"Earth to Andra. Earth to Anj—"

I jolted back to reality, turning my dazzling smile to my best friend as soon as the IG Live began.

"Kobe!" I squealed in pure joy. "You see this shit?" I yelled as we watched the view count go up on the shared screen of our impromptu IG live.

"Yeah, Boi" he said, white toothed smile beaming, slow, steady claps belying his barely contained excitement. "This is wild. Thirty-two thousand viewers already in the room...?" he said more as a disbelieving question rather than a statement. "And we still have three minutes before go time!"

Our IG lives were always lit, but the fact that it was looking like a D-Nice jam session during the pandemic was surreal.

"*Yo,* keep on coming in the room," I said, hyping up the new-comers. The energy was infectious and the chat was on fire. "I know it was last minute, but y'all showing the fuck out!" I screeched excitedly at the camera. "We are so excited for y'all to join us today!" I genuinely was in awe at how many of our followers joined with such short notice. Heart emojis flew across the screen.

"You reading these comments, Andra_B?" Kobe asked, speaking directly to me over the video feed, "We got some of our A1's online with us today, too."

"PERIOD!" I snapped my finger in appreciation of our dedicated followers who rode hard for Kobe and I. Always interacting, liking, sharing, and commenting on our stuff.

"You know we got some ride or dies at Gastrafrique!" I squinted at the small screen, moving in closer to shout out some folks and read a few comments from the chat out loud.

@Daddy_B_Right: Can't wait to see what the dynamic duo has to share with us tonight

"Thank you, Daddy_B_Right!" I smiled coyly, replacing the "D" sound in his name to seductively call him Zaddy. "We are about to get into it!"

@69Flavors_CreamPie: @Chef_Ko_Bae I hope whatever y'all sharing t'night includes you taking that damn shirt off!!!

@MzLeisha_Q: I 2nd that emotion

@Afrobeats_Live123: Nah we trying to get @Andra_B to show off them #goodknees again like she did outside @theselectatl in that sexy ass LBD last weekend

@ food_porn_minaj : Yess... that food had her ass all the way turnt. GOING FOR SUNDAY BRUNCH with my girls!

"Ooo Kobe! They lit-lit" I said staring dead into his eyes, wicked gleam in mine before gently egging him. "You taking your shirt off for the 'gram tonight, my boi?" I giggled when he shrugged his lips at me, giving me a deadpan face. My smile slipped a bit when I glanced at Kobe's chest, imagining him pulling the fitted black turtleneck over his perfectly chiseled chest. On camera. I shook the thought as quickly as it had come.

"You know... I just might take this muhfuckah off," he said, turning the dead pan for me off, turning on pure dark-chocolate charisma for our viewers, continuing, "If they keep this good energy going." The chat once again exploded with heart, eggplant, and fire emojis.

"Alright, alright! It's 7PM," I said, fanning and swooning, egging on the audience's reaction to Kobe. It was time to announce our good news. Break up some of the parties happening in our females and probably a few of our male followers' panties. "I'm sure all you good folks are ready to hear why we wanted y'all here today. You ready to get this *thang* started, Kobe?"

"Yep, yep. Let's tell 'em," he said sitting back in his seat, relaxed posture, fingers steepled and looking like sex personified. I watched him command the attention of the audience in amazement. He hated doing social media. Hated being in front of the camera, but our followers loved him. Yet, he was so humble.

I saw through his cool composure too. I knew Kobe like the back of my hand. He masked his anxiety about being on camera with his cool, laid-back demeanor, but I also could tell that he was bursting at the seams with excitement about what we were sharing with our audience on the live today. His tell was his west African accent. After years of being in the US it was barely detectable anymore. Except when he was excited. Then it was on full display. It was on full display tonight.

"First," he continued, "*Shot'out* to the big homie @Daddy_B_Right in the comments. My G, you've been *rock'un* with us since the beginning of Gastrafrique!"

"Right? Now that's a super fan." I interjected, nodding at Kobe.

He continued, "It's because of dedicated followers like you sharing your heritage with us, that inspires us to share our fusion blend of African American... I mean true African American, me from Ghana and Andra with her ties to East Africa, we get to share our blended heritage and love of Afro-fusion cuisine with you..." Kobe's words trailed as he looked proudly over at me.

I picked right up where he left off.

"Without further ado, we are proud to announce that Gastrafrique has grown to five million followers on IG, surpassing the number of followers of all food blogs in every category in the United States.

"And let's be clear. Not just for BIPOC founded food blogs, either," Kobe added proudly.

"Cheers to all of us African-Food Freaks." The chat went wild with excitement again. I beamed from ear to ear, and Kobe fist pumped, causing another flurry of emojis.

"We out here competing with the likes of Gordon Ramsey and shit!" he said, "And you guys know with that kind of fanfare, we're celebrating a multitude of offers now coming in to sponsor Gastrafrique. And none of this would have been possible without all of you." Another flurry of comments rolled up the screen before Kobe turned, giving me the floor.

And perfectly on queue, I bull horned my hands around my mouth and shouted, "We are now Brand ambassadors for Conde Nast! Link in bio BITCHES!"

"Yep. You heard right. Click the link in our bio for a special discount code for 25% off every luxury restaurant brand in the Conde Nast network. Courtesy of Gastrafrique."

"And that's not all!" I continued to yell excitedly, as I jumped to my feet for the next part of our announcement. I was glad for the 360 degree auto tracking tripod for my phone. I needed it to track my every movement as I did a full spin for the camera, struck a pose, and continued.

"We are also now brand ambassadors for Ivy Paaaaarrrrrrrkkk," I threw my hands up. Field goal. And the chat went literally apeshit!

Who would have known Gastrafrique, a little old Instagram page imagineered by me and my best friend Kobe over 10 years ago would be what it is today. It all started in his mom's kitchen, the day she taught us how to make fufu, a staple in West African cuisine.

This was back when you could only post pictures on Instagram and Baby, pictures we took. Our very first post was of that fufu, along with the full recipe in the comments. That post alone got five hundred likes. Definitely not viral, but impressive enough to light a spark.

We sat down on his mom's couch for hours racking our brains over what to call our page. All we cared about back then was making and eating good food, and capturing the vibe. It morphed into our ode to all things African Cuisine; the people, the culture and the tradition. That night, Gastrafrique was born on the fledgling, new Instagram.

Our first three posts were created that night too. Carousels didn't yet exist on the platform, so we posted three back to back photos with captions. The first was a picture of me in a velour Baby Phat sweatsuit pounding yams into a big wooden bowl. The next was of Mrs. Abara in a vibrant Ankara print headwrap giving me culinary direction. The last picture was of Kobe in a yellow Viktor Ikpeba soccer jersey, face rankled in pure bliss as he taste-tested the fufu he'd used to finger the delicious collard greens and oxtails Kobe's mom made for dinner that night.

Mine and Kobe's friendship was as strong now as it had been back then. We'd virtually grown up together on social media. We called ourselves the dynamic duo. Me, as Andra_B, socialite and food blogger extraordinaire. Kobe, 'aka' Chef_Ko_Bae, 'aka' Chef Kobe Abara, known internationally by his contemporaries as head Chef at Jah, one of Atlanta's only two Michelin starred restaurants.

Somewhere along our journey, we began making money from various sponsorships. Nothing like the money that was about to roll in from our Ivy Park and Conde Nast sponsorships, though. Gone were the days of us using our own money to eat at and critique four and five star restaurants around town. Now restaurants and other venues were paying us to just show up and talk about our experience on IG. Ten years and five million followers later, Gastrafrique was just getting started.

We'd wrapped up the live in less than twenty minutes. Kobe stepped out directly after to take a phone call. I was still in my guest bedroom, which doubled as our faux recording studio and my walk in closet. We both had similar setups at our own apartments so that we could record content whenever the mood called for it.

I was putting the finishing touches on my high bun, satisfied that I'd been able to wrestle the ass lengthed golden braids on top of my head. I was just about to slide on my signature Ruby Woo lipstick when Kobe came back in. He pulled up short in the doorway as soon as he walked in and asked, "Where you about to go?"

"I have a date," I casually said, looking in the mirror to check my full appearance.

"Obviously. You done switched up your outfit, your doo and everything. I was about to ask if you wanted to head over to mom and dad's with me to keep the celebration going, but I see you putting on your 'fuck girl' lipstick. Who's the mark tonight?"

"Um, first off watch ya' mouth," I said. One perfectly be-jeweled fingernail raised to cut him off. "Second, he's not a mark," I turned a matter of fact look in Kobe's direction, "I actually might like him. He's the same dude that took me to The Select for dinner last weekend to take pics under 'the most Instagram-able indoor garden'" I threw up air quotes, smiling at the slogan for the same place that was always popping up all over the 'Gram.

Kobe stared at me as I tugged the legs of my impossibly tight, black leather shorts down to a respectable level.

I started to ask Kobe what that look was all about, but decided against it. I was running late. Instead, I continued on about my date. "Dinner with 'that mark' and the subsequent review of 'that bar' is what got us to five million followers."

Kobe scoffed. "Andra I'm about a-thousand-percent sure it was that lil' ass dress you were twerking in at 'said bar' that got us over that milestone."

"Well, these red lips... these black leather shorts," I stuck out a pointed toe. "And these 4-inch red bottoms are about to get us at least a million more when I post the review of Prime Steakhouse tomorrow night!"

Kobe sucked his teeth at that.

"Ok. Second date? Dinner at Prime?" he rubbed his chin thoughtfully. "You know we got endorsement deals now, baby girl. You don't need to be out here scamming nigga's no more."

"Whelp," I giggled at his light-hearted jab, "A girl can never forget where she comes from..."

We both laughed at the running joke we'd had about me supposedly scamming dudes because I let them spend their money on me. Willingly, I might add. Knowing damn well I had no intentions of being with them. Back in the day, I used to run game and go on dates just so I could film content for the free ninety-nine. But we were living better now off legit sponsorships.

"And guess what, Kobe?"

"Oh damn. Here you go with the guess what. Can't be good."

"I'm just saying, this one might be the one," I shrugged. "You never know."

At that, his face relaxed, lips pressed together giving me his classic deadpan look when he doubted my sincerity. Then he folded over, gut busting laughter.

"Yeah right, this nigga bout to get took for a $600 dollar meal and stuck with blue balls."

"And on that note, I'm about to be late. You can see yourself out."

I grabbed my clutch and keys and headed towards the door. I paused briefly to yell back at him. "Let's set up a real celebration at your Mom's Saturday night. You know she is just as much the reason for Gastrafrique's success as we are. Love you boy." I blew a kiss at him and closed the door behind me.

Chapter 2 – Andra

♥

ON MY WAY TO the restaurant, I thought back on a couple of things that Kobe had said after our live. One being the fact that he genuinely thought that I was just in these streets not wanting to settle down for the sake of living my best life. That was so far from the truth. I was scared to settle down.

These men weren't loyal for starters. Then there were those playing musical pussy all up and down I-75 with secret families at home. The worst of the lot were the ones out here flexing on their coins, screaming for a girl like me to come pocket *check'em*. No scamming necessary.

Then there was that. Kobe's insistence on joking about that scamming shit bothered me. Funny how he only did that shit when I was about to go on a date.

We'd both heard about other food bloggers who'd really scammed some folks using the oldest trick in the book. Find a top notch spot. Make sure you book the reservation. Work with the restaurant to get them to comp the meal in exchange for pubbing them on your socials. Of course you couldn't let your date know any of this. Help run up the tab. Then fake like you have to go to the restroom, so you cut a side deal with the server. Server takes your date's credit card and pays for the meal, then refunds the cost back to you!

The seduce and mutherfuckin' scheme trick. I'd never done it before though. We never needed to do that though. Niggas spent on me freely and Gastrafrique has been sponsored for a while. Hell, most of our meals were comped by the establishments in advance because they knew we provided a beneficial service to them. If they provided great service and great food to us, they'd get a great review on Gastrafrique!

Keland, my date and rookie running back, had just signed with the Falcons. We'd been getting to know each other for about three weeks now, longer than most have lasted. We were going on our second official date. I'd been on a dating hiatus for about two months. Not even Kobe had known that. But a girl had needs. He was six feet of big, solid copper deliciousness and if he acted right, I just might give him the draws.

I weighed the idea of having this man blow my back out against dealing with a grown ass baby pouting in the A.M. when I inevitably sent him on his way... I know I'd told Kobe all that bullshit about this one being the one, but it was just that bullshit. I really just needed my back blown out. A bullshit story about 'it's me, not you...' or 'sorry but I'm just not ready for more' would have to do the trick to get rid of him before morning. I was pulling up to the valet by the time I'd made my internal decision to invite him up for drinks after dinner. Turned out, Keland's brother was the manager at Prime Steakhouse and he comped us with no cap. Ace of Spades bottle service on him.

———ele———

The shrill ringing of my phone was threatening to pierce my eardrum. I didn't want to risk pulling the cover from over my head, for fear that daylight would pierce my eyeballs. My right arm felt like it was led as I reached blindly towards the nightstand to pull the offensive piece of steel and glass under the cover to peek at the screen. As I was reaching, a broad arm reached around my waist and pulled me firmly towards the warmth of his body at the center of the bed.

"Whoa," I grunted, brain fully on alert now as the too much Ace of Spades and Coke induced cloud began to evaporate. Placing a firm hand on Keland's chest, I halted his attempt at a good morning kiss, opting to roll to the edge of the bed to answer my phone. "I have to take this," I whispered over my shoulder hoping he'd get the point. He didn't.

"Hello," I said in a hushed voice. It was Kobe.

Sounding like he'd been up for hours, Kobe greeted me in his usual boisterous baritone, tinged with Ghanaian slang, "Andra B, wake ya' *ahsss* up *gyul*! We gots more *celebrat'un* to do!"

Before I could pull the phone away from my ear. Away from Kobe's too loud voice, I had to quickly tuck it under my arm so he wouldn't hear Keland's loud ass trying to sweet talk me back under the covers.

Hell no! This nigga was definitely going to have to go with this shit. He did not have main man privileges to let his presence be known. For all he knew, my main man could have been on the other line. He was definitely about to get the speech and booted up out of here.

I placed the phone back to my ear in time to hear Kobe, whisper yelling, "Andra... I know damn well you did not let that lame nigga stay the night."

I hesitated before responding, looking over my shoulder at my bed mate. Stalling.

"That's none of your business. What's up and why are you calling me so damn early in the morning?" I hissed, eyes squeezing shut to stave off the impending headache.

"Morning? Andra it's Noon." Shit. Noon? Definitely too much Ace of Spades last night. And why did he have to yell so loud.

Kobe continued, "I just got an interesting call and I think you need to come to the crib ASAP!"

"Just tell me –"

"Get rid of the cornball and bring ya' *ahss*, Andra!"

CLICK. He hung up before I could make further arguments. *Rude!* On second thought, he'd just given me the best excuse to get rid of ol' boy.

"Hey... I'm so sorry," I put on my best soft girl seasoned voice, training my features to wide-eyed apology mode before turning to face Keland on the bed, "I have an emergency work situation with my partner that I need to go take care of." Oscar worthy performance if I did say so myself.

Chapter 3 —Kobe

♥

KNOCK. KNOCK.

I don't know why I rushed to answer the door. I knew it was Andra and she has a key. I shook my head at her showing up two whole hours later after I told this woman we had an emergency on our hands. I rush to greet Queen B. True to form, late without a care in the world. I opened the door expecting her to be dressed to the nines. Surprised that she wasn't. At least not by Andra's standards. The girl got dressed to go to the mailbox. Her motto had always been, 'if you stay ready, you don't have to get ready.'

Her hair was pulled back into a bun at the nape of her neck covered by a silk scarf and windshield sized shades covered her makeup free face.

As soon as I stepped out of the doorway, she breezed past me, making a beeline for my kitchen, helping herself to the fresh berry smoothie I'd just blended. I closed the door and turned, hands in my pockets as I watched her take over my shit. I should have been irritated with her. I actually was but for a different reason than her taking her time to get here. Her unkempt appearance spoke to a rough night, and all but confirmed that she and whatever the fuck his name was did more than have a few drinks.

I wiped a hand over my face, mentally checking myself, before following her to the kitchen. Arms re-crossed, leaning into the counter now, quietly taking in the freshly fucked aura she breezed in with.

After she fixed her smoothie, she turned around looking at me expectantly. Waving her hand at me like hurry up. "Damn Kobe. Are you going to tell me what was so urgent about this call?"

I didn't say anything immediately, letting the pause get under her skin, like her fucking ol' dude had gotten under mine. Petty. Sure, but I was just looking out for her. "Well Andra, I got a call this morning from a number," I paused again fishing my phone out of my pocket, "Out of California. The assistant of some big wig studio exec who represents the Food Network."

"Studio exec?" her face scrunched in confusion.

"Representing the Food Network," I repeated slowly, relishing the confused look on her face.

"So... they want us to guest appear on a show?"

She waved her hand up in rapid circles in my direction as she continued her efforts to prompt me to spill the news.

I shook my head, no. I unfolded and refolded my arms, urging her to guess again.

"Guest write for their blog?"

Again. No. This time I shifted to cross my other leg.

"Submit a recipe?"

Her face was screwed up in heated agitation as I shook my head no to every one of her guesses. I was enjoying torturing her too much.

"Dammit Kobe! Spit it out?" She stumped like a kid who didn't get their way.

Satisfied I'd successfully gotten under her skin, I finally answered. "They want Gastrafrique to host its own TV show series focused around African Cuis—"

"Our own TV show?" She cut me off. Bouncing up and down and hooting and hollering.

"Um, that's not it," I said, smiling at her antics. Sobering a bit she let me finish. "They also want us to open our own restaurant."

"Shut the fuck up!" She said, covering her mouth to staunch her surprise. You better stop playing with me!"

"Baby *gyul*, I'm not playing with you. As a matter of fact, I've been waiting on your slow ass to get here so we can call them back so they can give us both the details."

"Hurry up. Call them!" She fanned me to the living room to sit.

Once we were both settled on my couch. I did just that.

The phone only rang twice before the same chipper voice greeted me. She already knew who I was before I even stated my business for the call. I was low-key impressed.

"Mr. Abara, I've been waiting for your call back. Do you have Ms. Bainswright with you?"

"Ummm. Yeah. She's – "

"I'm right here. Call me Andra."

"Ok great. Andra, I'm Solita Morret, talent representative at The Food Network and I'm sure Kobe has given you the rundown on the two amazing opportunities we'd like to extend to Gastrafrique."

"Yes. He has. But please do give me all the details, again!" Andra sang into the speaker end of my cell phone, pursing her lips and rolling her eyes at me, still miffed at my withholding of details.

Because I'd already heard the spill, I just sat transfixed on Andra as she took it all in for herself. The excitement on her face mirrored mine during the original call.

Wait what?

The part Solita just said was not a part of the spill she had given me. Andra's pinched brow and shift away from my phone confirmed that she was just as surprised at the added info.

"Can you repeat that last part!" Both Andra and I said at the same time effectively cutting Solita's overly chipper ass off.

"Oh! Well yes.", Solita continued as if unphased. It's an amazing deal. A rather unorthodox one, but amazing all the same. The idea for both the tv show and restaurant were pitched to the network by an anonymous V.C. and the studio loved it. The V.C. –"

I cut in. "By V.C., you mean an anonymous venture capitalist?"

"Yes. He has provided a very generous production budget that will provide all travel, wardrobe and other expenses for an 8 episode first season. Also, for the complete buildout of the G.A.F. restaurant. That's what we've taken to calling it around here," she chuckled, "Along with operating expenses for three years -."

"Solita, all that sounds amazing and all, but let's get back to the part about the show being shot in Kenya," Andra said, cutting Solita off again

I was back in the conversation now and abruptly added, "And opening a restaurant simultaneously in Atlanta?..."

Solita laughed nervously. "Let me assure you both that you will be well compensated for everything. The client thinks that Andra's online personality will translate very well onto the tv screen and Kobe, it is well taken that your notoriety as head chef of a Michelin starred restaurant gives you unique qualification to lead your very own restaurant build out. There's opportunity for your own star. For your own restaurant... Well, Gastrafrique's restaurant, you and Andra, in partnership with the Food Network. What this means my friends, if you accept this offer, you two stand to be the first food blog of any kind to garner such a rich deal. The client wants to start filming the TV show as soon as possible on sight in Kenya. At the same time Mr. Abara, you will have carte blanche decision on location, décor, menu, staffing... The whole shabang. You will be fully funded to begin build out as soon as possible."

The call went silent. The deal was on the table. Andra and I were both speechless.

Finally, Solita quietly said, "I know I've given you both a lot to chew on." Another nervous giggle. "No pun intended. Just know that this is a really amazing opportunity to take the GAF brand that you both created into spaces that allow your followers to step off of social media and be immersed in the world of African Cuisine! I've sent everything that we just discussed to your brand email account. I hope that is ok."

"Y- Yes," I stated as if unsure of what our email address was, simultaneously trying to get a sense of how Andra felt about all of this. Nothing. She was still stuck, mouth wide open and in shock.

"Great. Within the email is also a contract. Please read through it and I'm sure you will see that it is written hugely in you guys' favor. Have your lawyer review it as well and Umm..." Solita's voice became unsure for the first time since she'd answered the call. She continued after a second or two, "The client will need you to confirm within one week or the deal is off the table."

With that the call ended.

Andra immediately snapped out of her trance and ran over to my open MacBook on the dining room table. She was midway through keying in my password before I was on her tail to check that email. She printed the contract and related documents, two copies, and we both sat down to read through. Neither spoke until we were both done.

Andra sat back, in deep thought, eyes sweeping my condo tentatively before settling them on mine.

"It's a bomb ass deal."

I couldn't even front. It was a great deal. Solita's voice echoing the same sentiment in her parting words on the call didn't even do 'how good of a deal' it was any justice. Yet, I was still full of apprehension.

"Who was this damn anonymous venture capitalist that she kept talking about? And why 'GAF'?" I asked, mimicking Solita's nickname for Gastrafrique

I had all these questions, but the real anxiety was around splitting up our team. She was my Gastrafrique's glue. Mine— My glue. I was selfish about her. Territorial about our friendship. The only time we'd ever been separated was the year after our high school graduation. And only because she threw a tantrum, insisting I go to culinary school in France.

Yeah, I know she's a grown woman and all but Kenya? By herself? And what about our IG following? @Gastrafrique was a team effort. We were a dynamic duo! Have been a dynamic duo since we were thirteen years old.

It was this very chemistry between us, that magic, that brought about this deal. This stupid deal was about to fuck up the chemistry. Fuck up the brand. *Right?* I was exhausted from the swirl of emotions roiling in my head.

"Anj, I don't know –"

"I want to do it," she said so quickly, cutting me off. Her eyes locked on mine, unwavering finality. "This is a perfect opportunity for us."

"Kenya though...? You want to go all the way to Kenya to film a show? Why? The internet is everywhere. Why do you gotta go to Kenya to talk about African food?" The more I talked, the dumber my questions sounded.

We'd been talking about African food and traveling across Africa for the better part of ten years. We both represented the two coasts. I was born in Ghana, West Africa and had the privilege to travel back and forth over the years on summer trips to visit my family. Andra had never had the opportunity to travel to Kenya, where her family, dad, was from. We'd had goals to go there together.

Selfishly, I wanted to go with her the first time she visited Kenya. To be honest, if she never went at all, Good. I was her family. And if she didn't go, she'd never feel the disappointment of possibly never finding her roots. Her dad.

We'd talked about it a million times before. I'd used being a chef in a world renowned restaurant as an excuse. I'd just not made the time in my schedule to visit the country that she was so connected to.

My resolve in not wanting to take this deal was beginning to crumble.

"Kobe, we wanted this," she said softly, hands splayed, "Under different circumstances, I know." She weighed her words, giving a quick chuckle, continuing "This is way more than partying in Nairobi, eating good, and feeding elephants and shit," she rushed, taking a deep breath before rambling on. "Gastrafrique will get a fucking tv show out of this." She flopped back, spent. Argument made.

I still had a little, albeit weak, fight left in me. "Yeah, and since we're talking about Gastrafrique. We'll be breaking its chemistry. What about our followers?"

"We'll figure it out. Like you said, the internet is everywhere. It'll take some planning, a little- a lot more effort to do our IG lives, but we've done them remotely many times before. Now we get to do it from two different countries. This is what we've been waiting for."

"Building a restaurant is a lot of work," I argued weakly. "Plus, I'm already a Michelin star chef -!"

"No, Boo. Jah and its owner have a Michelin Star. And now you'll have your own restaurant to take all the way to three stars.

Kobe, this is our time. Sure, five million followers is cool. The money we get from sponsorships... legit. But this? This is a once in a lifetime opportunity and I get to prove that just because I've never stepped foot in Kenya before, my connection there is real.

I hated when Andra talked like this. Since we were kids, she'd daydream about her father, wondering why he'd left her and her mom on their own. She'd get in her feelings, then would try to out Kenyan the Kenyan who'd broken her heart so long ago. She'd created a connection with his people out of a sheer need to feel like she belonged. She'd never admit it, but I knew her wanting to go to Kenya now was more of a need to connect with the father she didn't know. That I understood..

"Set up the appointment with the lawyer."

Chapter 4 – Andra

♥

WE WERE DOING IT.

After reviewing the full contract and all the supplemental documents Solita emailed with our attorney, the deal was ultimately sealed. Everything she'd said on the phone checked out. The benefits of taking the deal were heavily skewed in our favor. We had five days left to call Solita back with our decision. Kobe wanted to wait until after we broke the news to our families.

He'd already set up a dinner for us to celebrate Gastrafrique reaching five million followers at his family's house. That simple celebration was about to turn into, 'Surprise!'. I knew that his mother, father, brother, and sister-in-law would all be in attendance. The Abara's loved to entertain so I'm sure there would be others from Mr. Abara's medical practice ,as well as a few of Mrs. Abara's associates from the accounting firm from which she'd recently retired. They were so proud of their sons. They'd never miss an opportunity to celebrate them.

It was going to be like old times when Kobe and I were kids and neighbors. The Abara's would have these huge dinner parties every Saturday night. Mrs. Abara said the enormous dinners reminded her of being back home in Ghana.

My mother was always at work so she never came, even though she was invited to each one. I, on the other hand, was a fixture in the Abara household. They treated me just like one of their own kids. Kenji, Kobe's older brother, was now married and Mrs. Abara had a daughter-in-law. Still, she treated me like the daughter they'd never had.

The anxiety around the opportunity that Kobe and I'd been presented with was causing a rift between us. I don't know about him, it had me totally off. Snippets of memories past of how we got here would randomly pop into my head. Like the first time I ever went to Kobe's house. I remember it like it was yesterday. The fight we'd been in at school that day was a blur in comparison to meeting his family.

His was so different from mine. I was an only child and had been used to spending a lot of time with myself. I'd had very little adult supervision back then. It was usually just me, peanut butter and jelly sandwiches and re-runs of 'A different World.' Until I met Kobe and the Abara's.

At first I was envious of how nurturing Mrs. Abara was to her sons. But it was Mr. Abara's involvement in the everyday rearing of their kids that was foreign to me. He was equally engaged with them, from shooting hoops with them in the evenings to saying grace over every meal. He was so funny, too. I loved just being around them. I wanted to be a part of that so bad that one day it just naturally fell out of my mouth that my father was Kenyan.

Back then I had no clue about the vastness of Africa or how far Ghana was from Kenya. I had no concept of Ghana being on the west coast or Kenya being on its east. Hell, I had no concept of Africa being a continent at all.

Mrs. Abara gave me an entire geography lesson that afternoon. sucking her teeth as she often did when her spirit was vexed by something. *'What'ah they teaching you cheeldrun in school these days.'* I smiled at the memory. Kobe was embarrassed but Mrs. Abara didn't care. She kept right on fussing. her words though brash, felt like a warm hug to me though. I was included.

Her face would light up when she talked about Ghana. Kobe would be bored with her stories he'd heard a thousand times before and often would leave us in the kitchen while he, Kenji and Mr. Abara would shoot hoops in the driveway.

One such day, we were in their kitchen. She'd been teaching Kobe and I how to make this traditional fish dish from Nigeria. Hearing a story coming on, Kobe vanished. This time, instead of a story, she offhandedly asked, "Andra, are you going to Kenya to look for your father one day?"

I was frozen by her words. No one had ever asked me that before. My mother all but refused to talk about my father or his country. It felt as if she wanted to erase him from existence. Eventually, I stopped asking about him at all. Stopped thinking about him,

Unti Mrs. Abara asked that question. I felt her eyes on me when I didn't answer immediately. I was transported back to the last time I remembered seeing him.

*　ⅇℓℓⅇ　*

"Daddy, daddy, daddy!" I jumped up and down like I did every time my daddy came home. Daddy was gone so long this time. A whole month! Mommy said it was because he had to go home to take care of his family business. I don't know what 'business' is but I know it must be important because he was always going home. Mommy said he was going to take us when I get older! And each time, I'd jump up and down, pleading that four is older...

"My baby gourd," daddy yelled my nickname as he swooped down to pick me up and swing me around. I squealed and squirmed in a toothless grin as he tickled my neck with his nose. "Do you have gifts for me, Daddy?"

Mommy rolled her eyes, as she stood with her arms crossed in the entry way to the living room. "This girl is always asking for gifts," she said, looking like she had sucked on a lemon before smiling at me and daddy.

"Of course, I do," he said, looking down at me while scratching his brow perplexed, "But I don't know where they may be —"

"I do. I do," I cut him off while jumping up and down like a pogo stick, "It's in the suitcase!"

"Ahh..." he said as if I was the smartest girl ever, then reached around unzipping the suitcase that sat at his feet as he did every time we played this game. This time pulling out the most beautiful doll I had ever seen. It wasn't like any of the white Barbies that Mama would never let me get from Wal-Mart. "Here you go, ma'Baby! One that looks just like you! Brown butter toast!"

"Yep! Brown butter toast! Like me Daddy," I bounced up and down in excitement, tugging at the beautiful beads that adorned the dolls neck. The doll was as big as me and there were a lot of beads seemingly holding up the vibrant red, plaid scarf that wrapped around her body like a dress.

"Now go play with your warrior princess in your room while I talk to your mommy!

I did just that, took off like a lightning bolt to my room to play with my new doll. Just like always, Mommy and Daddy would go into their room to talk. Didn't sound much like talking to me, though. It was more like someone was slaying a howling, hissy cat. That sound always meant mommy would make blueberry and cinnamon pancakes in the morning. Yummy!!

This time was different though, after the cat died, they continued to talk. But it sounded like mad talking and Daddy was just as loud as Mommy and Mommy sounded like she was cry'n.

The next morning when I woke up, I bounded out of bed to make my way down to help mommy set the table for breakfast. She wasn't in the kitchen. I ran outside to the porch to see if Daddy was out there smoking one of his smelly cigarettes. He wasn't out there. I made my way down the hall to Mommy and Daddy's room and the door was closed but I could hear mommy still cry'n. I heard Aunt Vi's voice on the speaker phone sounding like she was ready to go fight somebody. "Where that Nigga at now?" she yelled.

Mommy yelled back, "Vi! You not listening! He did it already. He married that Kenyan Bitch –"

I stood there frozen not really knowing what a Kenyan Bitch was but I knew it was bad and I was scared. I couldn't understand the rest of what mommy was talking about because she kept yell'n, cry'n and cuss'n all tangled into mush. Kinda' like I was feeling on the inside. I ran and sat by the window looking out at the driveway waiting on Daddy while Mommy stayed in the room cry'n all day. That weekend was the last time either of us saw him. It was the day I realized that even good girls get left.

That day in Mrs. Abara's kitchen, I vowed one day I was going
to Kenya and it is also when I became a fanatic about all things
Kenyan cuisine. I was obsessed. It was the biggest fuck you I could
say to the spineless bastard who left my mother to raise me on her
own. "Yes, ma'am. I am." I said thoughtfully to Mrs. Abara's question Just as Kobe loped back into the kitchen to grab a Gatorade.

"What I miss?" he said, looking back and forth between me and
his mom.

Chapter 5 – Andra

♥

THE 40-MINUTE DRIVE FROM my midtown condo to the Abara's gave me plenty of time to second guess my ability to host an African-fusion food show. Sure, Kobe and I did it all the time on social media. Gastrafrique was basically our love letter to African cuisine. I knew a good *mshikaki* from a bad one and could dissect the ingredients in a *tsebhi* stew from a simple taste. After ten years, I was an expert in the culinary differences between east, west, north, south, and central African countries. Yet, I felt like an imposter going to Kenya to talk about African food.

Why did they want me to do it? I was just a bastard child of some random Kenyan guy. The most novice Kenyan cook would be more authentic.

Less than three days ago I virtually twisted Kobe's arm into agreeing to this deal. Yesterday... I was extremely excited about finally going to Kenya. Today, the gravity of it all hit me.

By the time I pulled up to the Abara's , Kobe's Range Rover was already parked out front of the expansive Italian style villa overlooking the historic Roswell mill. It was a far cry from the old Dixie Hills neighborhood in northwest Atlanta. where we grew up!

My mom still lived in the now heavily gentrified area. My same childhood home, remodeled many times over the years, sat perfectly in between other half million dollar homes. Mom had made a great investment back in the early two thousands when you could buy a house on the same street for less than forty grand.

Funny thing is, Kobe and I grew up in the hood and didn't even know it...

The thought brightened my spirits a bit as I pulled in right behind Kobe. I still did a quick check in the mirror, making sure I hadn't messed up my makeup during my walk down my memory lane. Still flawless.

Within seconds I was ringing the doorbell as a courtesy, before just walking in like family. I was greeted by the aroma of Jollof Rice and a full on West African style party. I spoke to the few guests already gathered in the living room on my way to the kitchen. Everyone was festive, no doubt from the strong potions from Mr. Abara's wine cellar he'd built last year. I was on a mission to find the lady of the house and her son.

I grabbed one of the many aprons on hooks just outside the swinging doors and had it over my head, securing it around my waist by the time I stealthily walked up to her, holding up a finger to my lips to silence an onlooking Kobe.

Her back was turned to the pot she was stirring, undoubtedly filled with oxtail stew. I threw my arms around her waist planting a big wet kiss on her warm cheek. She jumped. Startled at first, then quickly spinning to smother me in her hefty arms.

"There goes my girl!" she said, holding me out at arm's length with the biggest, warmest smile I'd seen in a while. "Let me take a look atcha' child." And as was our ritual, I struck a bombshell pose, causing her raucous laughter. Customary exaggerated sucking of her teeth, before she nudged her head in her son's direction. "A supermodel she be. Ain't she Kobe!"

"Mama, please don't gas her up," he said, through a half smile that didn't quite reach his eyes. As soon as my eyes met his, he shifted them away, focusing heavily on the red onion he was skillfully dicing. My eyes narrowed at the slight. I blew it off after he turned to the sink to rinse the knife he'd been using off, realizing he'd been slicing more than red onions. There were chiles and tomatoes, too. Pepper sauce. That could only mean one of those pots on the stove had greens in it. YES.

I had all but forgotten about Kobe's distant behavior. Until he said, back still turned, "Better be careful not to get any of that stew on her dress. You see she done showed up in a custom dashiki print mermaid skirt for a simple family dinner." I heard him mutter, 'she a super star, now' under his breath.

Oblivious to the shade her son was giving me, Mrs. Abara burst out in laughter at Kobe's joke. I made a mental note to check his ass later.

When Ms. Abara turned back to the stove, I mouthed a quick, "Have you told them yet?" in Kobe's direction. He shook his head no. That explained why I was the only one dressed up. It was just a regular family gathering at the Abara's. Ok, so even if they didn't know about the announcement we'd be making, Kobe knew as well as anyone, I was always going to show up and show out. Even more of a reason to check his ass.

Kobe was out of order. But upon further consideration, I knew my best friend . I knew he was stressed about this whole ordeal. So was I. But it was too late to back out now. We'd agreed to accept the offer and would be sharing the news in just a few minutes with his family.

"What's all this commotion?"

I followed the sound of the booming voice to the kitchen door. I had moved to throw my arms around him before anyone else could react to the presence of Kobe's dad .

He acted like I'd knocked the wind out of him, squeezing me back equally as tight. "*Oh-Oh!* Our third child done made an appearance," he chuckled. "Child we haven't seen you in a *montha'* Sundays," he joked.

"Mr. Abara, it hasn't been that long, has it?" I asked, trying to do fake math on my fingers knowing full well it had been well over a month since I'd made my way to Roswell to see them.

"Girl I done told ya' a million times, stop calling me Mr. Abara. My name is Ayi. I am not that old."

Mrs. 'A' sucked her teeth over the pot she'd gone back to stirring. A snicker escaped from my lips. The shade of it all.

Unphased, Ayi Abara shewed a hand at his wife then held it up to his face, pretending to whisper And doing a horrible job at it. "Now that one," he twisted his lips, "Now she old. It's Mrs. Abara for her."

"Naw, now., Mr. A.," I sassed in mock defense. "You gonna' get off that one. I'll fight a brick about her," I said laughing full out at our familial banter.

"That's right. Girl power! " Mrs. Abara piped. "Don't you worry about that old fool, Andra. It's time to eat."

With a flourish, she picked up the fancy dish that she'd ladled the stew in moments before and carried it out of the kitchen to the table in the formal dining room. And just like when we were teenagers, we grabbed the other dishes of succulent food and filed out like baby ducks. There were enough bowls, platters, condiments and serving utensils to feed a whole village on that table.

The familial bond and sincere joy I felt when around them was palpable. They couldn't get rid of me if they tried!

And just like that, dinner was served. Guests were coming to the table from all directions. I don't know how they knew the food was ready. Nobody made an announcement. They just knew.

Everyone took their seats around the table except Mr. Abara. As was the tradition, he kicked off the dinner by telling a story. Kobe groaned. Kenji slumped. I leaned in. This one was from his youth. It was about being grateful and appreciative of what you have. His dinner stories were akin to a prayer or blessing. Nobody interrupted the prayer, but when he finally exclaimed, "Dig in," the whole table went up in collective, 'whews,' 'damns,' and good-natured laughter and dug in.

During dinner, Mrs. Abara and I talked about fashion, something we both loved. I was laughing about her retelling of a mishap she'd had at Macy's the other day when Kobe stood, clinking his glass to get everyone's attention.

The room hushed and all eyes were on him. I smiled cautiously at him. He was about to break the news.

"As you all know, my best friend Andra and I started a little unknown Instagram page a few years back. Mama, you know better than most, because we started out sharing pictures of dishes you taught us to cook," he paused to nod at her.

"Oh yes," she beamed at her son, "Those first few meals were rough!" The room filled with laughter. Including Kobe this time. I was glad to see him smile.

"It was Andra's idea to begin posting then and much later when I finally learned to plate food. She always had a knack for making whatever we posted look like a culinary masterpiece. My major contribution was suggesting that we start taking pictures of other folks' food too, I couldn't have all the shine," he laughed wryly. He brought his hand to cup his chin. Pausing momentarily, continuing almost as if realizing something for the first time. "You know, we never strayed far from our original goal of just tapping into our collective heritages. That goal allowed us to gain a sense of self first. It allowed us to draw parallels between traditional African cuisine and food of all cultures being whipped up at some of the most prestigious restaurants in the city."

His eyes finally met mine. "Today we are proud to announce that not only has our passion transcended to a lucrative social platform for like minded foodies, but today the world has taken notice. Gastrafrique -,"

"Getcha freak on," Mr. Abara said, raising his glass and chuckling at the phrase he'd often yell out whenever someone said Gastrafrique.

"Hush, Ayi! Let the boy finish," Mrs. Abara scolded her husband across the table, eyes back on her son to hear more of what he was getting at.

Kobe smiled wistfully, shaking his head , continuing, "We are proud to announce that Gastrafrique has reached 5,000,000 followers this week."

Kobe's father always the comedian said, "What? You mean to tell me that you can make some money by taking pictures of your food? Sign me up baby. I'm quitting my practice!" More laughter, but it still had not reached Kobe's eyes. I'd mentally gone down a rabbit hole, trying to figure out how to cheer my friend up and almost didn't hear him when he called my name.

"Andra," he called again, "Will you stand up with me please,"

I did, picking up my wine glass too. Holding his stare across the table.

"Over the years you all have watched my friendship with Andra grow. Not only has she been a friend but she has been my rock, accepting a scrawny, black as night African kid with a thick accent. I had no friends in these Atlanta streets and she took me in. Because of her tenacity and daring to be different, not caring what anyone thought about it, she helped me grow. Her love of her own African and African American heritage showed me that it was OK to love and be proud of mine before Afrobeats and *Black Panther* made it cool. She's the reason Jah got that Michelin star that everyone loves to say is mine. And she has used that marketing degree from Spelman to solidify Gastrafrique as a household name in luxury culinary and foodie circles. Because of her, we just accepted a deal expanding the Gastrafrique brand, where Andra will be traveling in the next couple of weeks to Kenya to film the Gastrafrique TV show."

Everyone in the room clapped at that. But simmered down when I clanked my glass like Kobe had done to get their attention moments before. Kobe's words had taken me by surprise, but he conveyed way more than adulation towards me in them. For a moment he was that little scrawny new kid in middle school and I was that little girl who'd felt so alone until he came along. And I would have fought the world for him.

I swiped at the moisture collecting in my eyes. "Kobe is only being humble. Without his creations and remixes of your dishes, Mrs. A," I also nodded my head at her, "We wouldn't have had anything to photograph and post. So, while I'm off working on the show, you all should be so proud that Kobe will be here holding down the fort working to launch the Gastrafrique restaurant!"

The room went up in applause again. Through the congratulations and claps, I found Kobe's eyes. I gave him the best crinkle faced smile I could muster and said directly to him. "Needless to say, I'm so very proud of you. And I'm scared shitless to be without my best friend, too." His smile reached his eyes for the first time

I'd seen tonight, before he lowered his head to blink away his own tears.

Chapter 6 – Andra

♥

NOT LONG AFTER KOBE made the announcement to his family, I said my goodbyes to head over and break the news to my mom. He walked me out, neither of us saying much.

I broke the awkward silence first. "Those were some really nice words you said about me in there," I smiled up at him hoping he'd do the same. At first he looked away, shoving his hands deep in the pockets of the close fit jeans he wore, a signature sign he was holding back words or emotions.

It gave me a moment to study his dark features washed in the glow of the many lights that lined the circular drive. I'd always thought he was beautiful. It wasn't often that I got to openly stare at him. Normally if he'd caught me staring, he'd say something silly to make me laugh to take the attention off himself.

That little skinny kid had glowed up into the most kind-hearted man I knew. Sometimes I thought he was too good a person for the likes of me.

His eyebrows drew together in anguish as he lowered his head again to hide his emotions.

My heart broke a little. "Ah bestie it's only for a little while," I tugged at his sleeve, coaxing his hand out of his pocket to intertwine our fingers, "Stop acting like you gon' miss me."

A sigh escaped his lips, before one corner turned up slightly in a lopsided smile. I was just glad he wasn't stone facing me any longer. Felt even better when he pulled me into him. He wrapped his arms around me squeezing like he didn't want to let go.

We stayed like that for a while. We rarely hugged, stemming all the way back to high school because of all the accusations from our classmates about us being more than just friends. The last time he openly held me like this was during that same time after our junior prom. We'd double dated. He with Carmel Dobson and I had been asked to go by a senior and one of Kobe's teammates on the basketball team.

From the moment we'd all loaded into the limo, the vibe was off. I could feel scorching heat radiating in my direction from Carmel. And Kobe, her date, was shooting daggers at Luke when he thought no one was looking.

During prom, my date had disappeared on me and when I went in search of him, I found him balls deep in Sinead Gleeson's skanky ass on the back stairwell behind the gym. Apparently it was supposed to be me that he was going to fuck on those stairs and Kobe had gotten wind of it and told Luke he would beat his ass if even thought about touching me.

When I ran out of the gym, Kobe left his date Carmel in the makeshift ballroom to come find and comfort me. Tonight, he held me just as tight.

He rested his chin on top of my head and spoke for the first time since we'd walked out of his parents' house. "I meant every word back there. It's just... this is a lot. This is all moving so fast." I squeezed him a little tighter. He sighed again. "I'm sorry for being rude to you tonight. Just been a little fucked up in the head."

I nodded my understanding into his chest, saying between sniffles, "You know you may have to do some of the lives by yourself, right?"

He verbally groaned at the thought.

He couldn't stand all the attention on him. Kobe was an extreme introvert at times, only extroverted when commanding a kitchen. Though, his quietness, combined with his exceedingly good looks, drove women crazy. Our female followers were drawn to him like a moth to a flame. And still the only time he'd engage at all in front of the camera was if I were there with him. He'd ride the wave of my over-the-top nature. Apparently it worked for us.

"The ladies are going to love having you all to themselves for a little while," I teased, finally getting him to laugh out loud.

"You might be right, my friend," he said, squeezing me tighter before releasing his grip and opening my car door. "Go ahead and get in. Call me and let me know how the convo with your mom goes."

I parked on the street in front my mom's gallery. She usually had a lot of foot traffic, even this time of night so I was surprised to see that it was virtually empty. The doors were still unlocked, so I knew she was still there. Probably in the back of the storeroom.

The gallery space was beautiful, as elegantly curated as Evelyn Bainswright, the owner and my mother. I navigated the maze of angled walls, admiring some of the pieces on display, as I made my way to the offices.

I heard chatter in the back where I was headed, finding my mother at one of the desks used for curation of pieces that people brought in to be put on exhibit. Her heeled feet were kicked up on the desk as she threw her head back laughing at something my uncle Trey had said. I was shocked to see him and my aunt Vi, my mother's twin sister. The two sisters were identical in appearance, but they were night and day in every other way.

Aunt Vi and Uncle Tre looked to be dressed up, probably to go to dinner or a show in town. They lived in Woodstock, about an hour north of the city. They were all enjoying a glass of wine. When I walked up to them. Neither seemed surprised to see me. Undoubtedly the door chime and my heels on the polished hardwood floors preceded me.

"Andra, I knew it was you from your heavy steps," my mother's words mocked, never one to miss an opportunity to point out the fact that I wasn't a perfect 5'6" and 135 pounds like her. One day she would learn that thick thighs and plump asses were in.

"Ok. No warm up necessary before throwing your first jab tonight." I said, waving her off. My quick witted come back, words dripping in sarcastic sugar, came naturally. I'd learned from the best. I was used to her bite.

"Did I call it, Vivi?" My mom continued, unphased by my counterpunch.

"Yes, *heffa*. You called it," Aunt Vivian said, throwing a flitting apologetic look in my direction, silently apologizing for my mom's subtle shade. Nevertheless, pulling a ten out of the small clutch, handing it over to my mother.

"It's me," I said with exaggerated cheer. Jokes on me. I made my way over to Aunt Viv and Uncle Tre first, giving both hugs before making my way around the desk to kiss my mother on her smooth upturned cheek. We weren't really into the touchy-feely thing, so I wasn't surprised when she didn't pull me into a hug. As

I straighten from the kiss, smoothing my long skirt down my aunt VI chimed in, "Don't you look cute."

My mother was next adding, "Yeah. Your get up is interesting," she said, waving her hand up and down my body as if I were one of the pieces of art on display. "I can tell you've been with Kobe and his family. Let me guess. Family dinner?"

"Yes," I piped silvery, remaining cordial despite her slick comment about 'them folks always eating' that followed. "As a matter of fact, I was, and that leads to why I'm here. I have good news," I bounced on stilettoed toes. Why the hell I was acting like a nervous kid, was beyond me. Clearing my throat, I continued, "I wanted to stop by and share it with you."

"Let me guess. You tried a new African restaurant for your 'little' social media thing?" she said, placing her hands under her chin looking at me expectantly. I paid her no never mind as she always threw shade whenever Gastrafrique was mentioned.

Even though it paid my college tuition and afforded me a swanky downtown condo *sans gratis* from her, she looked down on my line of work. Well not so much my line of work, more so the subject of said work. Over the years I had learned to tune her out and only came to tell her now because of the length of time that I would be gone out of the country.

"Gastrafrique is hardly little, mother," I cut my eyes at her.

"Oh," my mother said, satisfied she'd gotten under my skin with that 'little' comment.

"As a matter of fact, we just hit 5,000,000 followers. "I smiled sweetly at her. Satisfied I'd momentarily wiped the smug look off her face. Neither of us released the eye lock we were trapped in.

Noticing the rising tension between mother and daughter, Aunt Viv cleared her throat quickly, quirking her eyebrows up at Uncle Tre. Before interjecting. "Five million followers, Andra. That is something! My little Instagram page only has about 200 on it." She smacked her slender thigh chuckling. Uncle Trey pulled her deep into his side. "That's ok baby, You got your biggest follower, right here."

My mom made a gagging sound in the background.

Aunt Viv scowled at her sister as Uncle Tre turned to me. "That's amazing, baby girl. Congratulations." He then softly reminded his wife they needed to go if they were going to be on time for the play they were in town to see.

I'm sure my mother's dispassionate interest in what was going on around her had something to do with running them off too.

"So, what's the 'and'?" My mom asked with passive interest. Everyone trained their eyes back at me to hear what else I had to share.

"Well. Kobe and I were presented with an offer we couldn't refuse…"

My mother's face twisted, as she openly rolled her eyes at the mention of Kobe's name. Two things she hated in this world, anything connected to Africa and men. Kobe had two strikes. I ignored her sour demeanor, turning my attention to Aunt Vi because I knew what I said next was going to gut punch my mother.

"Kobe and I have been offered a tv and restaurant deal for Gastrafrique. I'll be flying to Kenya to film the show."

"Oh. Girl, that's fabulous!" Aunt Vi erupted, snatching me into a full-on embrace. My uncle's deep voice mirrored her excitement in his second congratulations. And before I could turn to my mother her nasty words stopped me in my tracks.

"Girl stop," she hissed, waving a dismissive hand at the news I'd just shared. "I know you're not flying to some third world country to film some low budget TV sho-"

"Evvie!" My aunt screeched, cutting her sister's harsh words off. "This is your child! You should be happy for the girl!"

Evelyn Bainswright got super petty, downright nasty any time I talked about going to Africa. She acted like my passion and career choice was a personal affront to her. As if I were choosing it over her. In some ways I was. I hated how color-struck and boujie she could be sometimes, absolutely abhorring anything African. At least that's what she portrayed to the world. I knew deep down; she hated every vestige of my father. And took that shit out on me..

"Tsk," my mother kept going, "Evvie, my ass... You've seen those raggedy ass Nigerian movies playing at the braid shop. Cheap. Low budget. You and your little boyfriend Kobe could record that mess with your cellphones. Probably, be much better quality." She singularly laughed at her own joke, while I quietly seethed, but Aunt Vi turned all the way up when she saw the hurt look on my face.

She moved in on my mother so quickly, open hand aimed straight for her face but was yanked back and pinned to Uncle Tre's side before she reached striking distance. Her body rigid with anger as she said, "Evvie, that's some cold shit you just said to your child... But you've been a cold bitch ever since that stunt you tried to pull with her daddy backfired on your stupid ass—"

"Let's go, Vi!" Uncle Tre's voice cut through the air like a knife as he began pulling his wife towards the exit.

"Yeah. Let's go Vi... Best get on up out of here cause your hubby said so!" My mother yelled after them. As they passed, I could hear Uncle Trey whisper, "That is not your business to tell," before they disappeared out the door. When I turned to my mother, she was clutching at her neck as if Aunt Vi had physically choked the shit out of her. I turned on my heel, leaving her where she stood.

Chapter 7 – Andra

T HE ONE THING MY mom surely could do, was piss me off. I sat in my car outside of the gallery. My forehead rested on the cool steering wheel so I could calm down. She better be glad she holds that title because I would have chosen violence on a less esteemed individual. I wanted to smack the smirk off her face. It was nasty and vile and perfectly conveyed her disdain for anything that I did that was not influenced by her oh so perfect pedigree.

I looked up, surveying the darkness of the side street. It was as dark as my mood. All the businesses were closed except for the bar at the end of the block. I didn't have to worry about foot traffic walking by looking at the crazy woman stewing over some bullshit her mom said in her car on a lonely, dark block.

I contemplated going to the bar to have a few drinks to calm my nerves. I really didn't want to be around a whole lot of people, though. I certainly didn't want to entertain any small talk. I didn't want to go home to sit in my feelings either.

Fuck, I didn't want... I didn't know what I wanted right now aside from screaming at Evelyn Bainswright. I was too much of a respectable daughter to do that. So, I decided to do what I always did when my emotions were in free fall and I didn't want to burden Kobe with my bullshit.

Moments later, I clicked the push button to start my car. Plan for the rest of my evening taking shape. I made a left at the light onto Peachtree Street. Just before jumping onto the 17th street bridge, then south on I-75 in the direction of my condo, I activated the voice control built into the custom sound system.

"Call Keland," I spoke into the embedded microphone in the visor of the car, glad I'd never gotten around to blocking his number as I'd planned to do when he left my apartment the other morning. He'd been calling and texting non-stop. Men were simple like that. Leave them on red, take a few days to return their calls... they'd be up your ass and trying to cuff you within a week. And just as I knew he would, he answered on the first ring.

"There she is," he said, words honey dipped and oozing off his tongue, "I was beginning to wonder if you had forgotten about a brother."

I rolled my eyes at his unnecessary words. I fought off the urge to tell him to calm down. We'd seen each other less than a week ago. I needed something from him, and didn't want to give off that kind of energy. Instead, I ignored his words and quietly, but firmly stated, "My house. Thirty minutes," and ended the call.

By the time he got there I'd already removed all my clothes and poured myself a glass of wine. I downed the contents quickly, feeling the heat in my core. Another kind of heat instead of the rage that was running through me. I had selected a bad bitch playlist including Saweeti, Megan the stallion, City Girls, and any other hot girl currently making music that matched my fuck every-body mood. The mix was chopped and screwed, making even the most upbeat of songs slow and seductive. I set the volume on my surround sound low, but loud enough to dissuade unnecessary banter. It was giving sensory deprivation.

My condo apartment was located on the 10th floor, at the end of the hall so I had no issue leaving the front door ajar, cracked just enough so Keland would know to come right in. I'd extinguished all the lights in the living space, leaving a single candle burning just inside the interior of my bedroom. It was an open floor plan, so he was safe from bumping into walls or obstructions on the floor. And just like a moth, he was drawn to my golden flamed honey pot.

"Oof," he uttered, breath releasing from his chest the moment he stepped into my room. It was exactly the reaction I expected as I lay face down, ass up, pussy angled right at him and on full display. I watched him in the floor length mirror opposite the bed.

His dick swelled in his pants. He was held captive in the doorway as his eyes raked over my ass. The round cheeks highlighted by the flickering light of the candle. My knees were spread, so he could see my fingers stroking in and out of my shining slit.

Mmm he was ready. Instead of calling him over, I popped my lower back ever so slightly to the slow, punchy beat playing in the background making my ass cheeks vibrate for him. That was the only invitation he'd get. He didn't hesitate.

"You sexy, mother fucker," he said low in his throat, sharp intake of breath hissing between his teeth . I heard rather than saw his belt and pants clamber to the floor after he toed his shoes off and his socks went with them. Instead of crawling to join me on the bed, he kneeled at its edge, firmly clasping my hips in his huge hands, and pulled me to him, diving in face first. His erect tongue slid into the puckering of my ass. He licked and sucked. My pussy felt neglected, so I slipped two fingers into my wetness. When he had his fill of my ass, he slipped his face down further, meeting my fingers where they moved in and out of my pussy slowly. Tantalizing. Knowing he wanted his tongue there; I pulled each finger out and reached further between my legs to feed them to him. One by one he sucked each digit clean.

"Mmm," he moaned when I pulled the last finger from his lips. "It tastes like vanilla buttercream." He dipped his head even lower, angling his body so he was looking up at my pussy so he could catch my swollen clit between his lips.

"Ahh," my body jerked from the pleasure of his tongue.

He sucked firmly, flicking his tongue back and forth and igniting a million nerve endings in that small button of pleasure. I wanted to moan his name and tell him how good he made me feel, but I wouldn't. No talking. Just fucking. I rocked my hips back and forth over his tongue. My abdomen tightened. Warm tingling pressure building.

To keep myself from erupting around, in, *on* his hot, wet mouth, I reached for the condom. I'd already taken it out of the side table. I was still face down with my ass in the air so I had to reach behind me to hand him the gold foil package. Once he took it from my fingers, I left my wrist in a handcuff position.

He fully understood the assignment, turning my pussy loose from the lip grip he'd had on it. He ripped the square packet and donned the condom at lightning speed, ready to sink his juicy dick between plump cheeks forged from a million squats.

As soon as I was sure he was wrapped up, I allowed my left arm to follow the same path as my right, offering both arms to him for leverage. He was being granted 'Mr. Officer' privileges and had full permission to beat my pussy up. No talking. Just fucking. I needed to be fucked into forgetting the red, hot rage stoked by my mother's dismissal earlier. I needed to be fucked into submission. Skin to skin warfare.

We went at it like battling Olympians for at least an hour. I came at least three times to his two before we were both spent. The comforter and flat sheet were suspended between the foot of the bed and the floor, neither of us caring to cover our naked bodies. It was too late for modesty.

I didn't have to ask him to leave, as the time was nearing eleven PM and he had a four am practice in the morning. I saw him out. This time remembering to mute, not block his number in case I needed his services again.

Chapter 8 – Andra

♥

IT WAS HARD TO believe two weeks had already gone by. Kobe and I had been bombarded with more paperwork and endless calls from several people from the network. One of the calls was from my own personal concierge that took detailed notes on my diet, flight preferences, personal style, clothes, and shoe sizes. Even my under-garment sizes were taken.

I was getting annoyed with all the questions but then he explained that the studio would be taking care of my every need; living arrangements, transportation and food. That included a full wardrobe, so I kept every complaint to myself.

Today was the day I'd fly to Kenya. Kobe and I sat in his car for a while after he'd pulled his Range into the dropoff lane at the international side of the airport. Neither of us said much on the way.

"Well my bestie, I guess we're doing *thees shiit.*" Kobe said after a while of us just sitting there staring out the window.

My eyes were trained on the automatic doors of the terminal. They must have opened and closed a hundred times and twice that number of cars had zipped in and out of the dropoff lane before I trained my eyes on Kobe. He stared at me patiently from the driver's seat. Again filling the silence.

"You know... we could just jump right back on 285 and head back to the crib." He smiled wistfully, putting a voice to the exact thoughts in my head.

I smiled pensively, slowly releasing the breath I'd been holding. "Yeah, but you know this bad bitch isn't backing down from a little old trip to a land she ain't never been; where she *heard* that they got rogue elephants that'll run up in your village and stomp your ass out ..." I let out a nervous laugh to mask my false bravado. It was the first time we both laughed together since deciding to take the deal.

Catching my vibe, he chimed in, both scrunching our faces, shaking our heads profusely as we said in unison, "*We ain't neva sked*!"

"*Bone Crusher*!" He yelled, reaching over, pulling me clean across the console into the second hug we'd shared in as many weeks.

"You got this, Andra B!" He let out a deep sigh, releasing me back to my seat, "As you said, this is the moment we've been waiting for."

He was also talking about the Gastrafrique restaurant, the reason he was simply dropping me off at the airport instead of parking and walking me to the security checkpoint. The execs at the studio called a last-minute meeting with him about the restaurant so he'd have to go soon to make it back up to 17th street where the Food Network headquarters were. *In rush hour traffic.* If it wasn't such a lucrative deal with so many moving parts, I'd swear they were intentionally trying to separate us...

I reached for the door handle, but Kobe quickly reached for me again, grabbing my chin. His eyes were on my lips as he turned my face to meet his. Our lips were mere inches apart. The warmth of his breath singed my cheek as he whispered, "Go make me proud, Andra."

I was disoriented by his closeness but couldn't pull away. My eyes now fixed on his parted lips. He moved ever so slightly towards me.

BOOM. BOOM.

I snatched back. The officer beating on the window broke the trance. I grabbed my purse and retrieved the small carryon bag that held my MacBook and other travel necessities, opened the door and stepped out to the curb. Kobe popped the trunk and handed me my small suitcase.

I wrapped myself around his body like a child getting dropped off at daycare for the first time, already feeling a sense of separation anxiety. Any traces of the longing I'd seen in his eyes just moments before, gone. Pulling back, he pecked me on my forehead. I peeked up at him and smiled before sadly saying, "Nigga we 'bout to be famous."

He replied, voice thick with emotion, "Niggah, we already *fam-iss...*"

By the time I landed in Nairobi, I'd memorized the full packet and itinerary provided by the studio. The first season of the Gastrafrique tv show, yep there was a plan for multiple seasons, was focused mainly on Kenyan cuisine but on-air interviews had been set up for me with restaurateurs, cultural trend setters, owners, as well as patrons of local hot spots, and a host of celebrities from the region. and my mind was reeling from the insane amount of information in the packet provided; names of the film crew, biographies of each person to be interviewed. I worked my ass off on the long flight to know everything in it before touching down in Nairobi. Even studied the etymology of each name so I wouldn't fuck up a single one.

I was prepared, but my nerves were still getting the best of me.

I was exhausted by the time I landed. Thank you Jesus the studio had put me in First Class, Delta One even for the first leg of the trip, otherwise my back would be screaming on top of the mental and physical fatigue of the long flight.

Jomo Kenyatta International airport was straightforward to navigate. I was surprised to hear so many people speaking English around me. All the signs were in English, too. I had tried to learn Swahili over the years, but having no one to practice with left me with only a few basics for greetings and asking for directions. I'm glad, I wouldn't need to ask for directions tonight.

I'd made my way outside to ground transportation, remembering the instructions in the itinerary. There would be a driver to meet me as soon as I stepped out of the Airport. Yet, I was still unnerved when a strong, pristinely manicured hand grabbed my wrist. By the time I realized what was happening, he was bending over ever so slightly to press his lips to the back of my hand.

For the second time in less than 48 hours, I stood mesmerized, gaze locked on a beautiful African man. Both men, Kobe and this one, had butterflies flapping in my stomach. Kobe stirred them when he almost kissed me. I think. I hadn't yet, didn't know if I should even process that yet. This one had the hairs on the back of my neck buzzing with electricity from his sheer presence alone.

He was fine. Deep espresso skin glowing under the overhead lights, dressed in a body defining suit that appeared to be laser cut just for him.

"*Habari*, Ms. Bainswright," he said in a formal, deeply accented tone, more British than Kenyan.

"I am Okiyo Bamdi, the transportation liaison for—" He gave a nearly imperceptible pause, clearing his throat before continuing, "Assigned to you."

Transportation? The rippling muscles under his suit screamed bodyguard.

The protective hand he placed in the small of my back as he led the way to the back passenger door of the waiting black Denali, thrilled. Once I was safely inside, he circled the back of the SUV and climbed onto the backseat beside me. Ok. Shouldn't the transportation liaison be in the driver's seat? My attention pulled momentarily as I noticed for the first time someone else was in the driver's seat.

Catching my perplexed look, he cocked a brow in my direction, dryly stating, "I am your transportation liaison, not your driver, Ms. Bainswright." His cool demeanor worked to cool the heat he'd spurred in my uterus all the way down. I did not do pompous or dry ass men. I don't care how good he looked in his three-piece suit. Apparently he didn't 'do' me either. His impassive face paid more attention to straightening the cuffs of his jacket and what was going on out the window than me.

Never being one to cower, I continued, "And what exactly does a transportation liaison do?" I asked cocking an equally cool eyebrow.

He turned his head slowly to meet my curious gaze then he smirked just barely before stating, "I liaise." Hard stop. Period. He left me there on the seat next to him, bemused and blinking. Obviously done with the conversation, he tapped the partition and commanded,. "To the suites, Deké." And we were off.

For the next 30 minutes we rode in silence. It gave me the opportunity to take notice that people drove on the left side of the road in Kenya. And Nairobi at night was magnificent. It was a very modern city, skyscrapers dotting the skyline in twinkling lights. The multitude of tall buildings were emblazoned with logos of many major corporations; Google, Amazon, Microsoft. The big tech companies were here in force.

As we slowed, pulling off the expressway into a more secluded, residential neighborhood., *The bodyguard*, I'd aptly named him in my head, leaned forward and pointed up the hill that we were traversing slowly. "You will be staying in a two-bedroom apartment in the heart of the Westlands," he stated, looking over at me to ensure that I understood. I understood him just fine, even with his thick English brogue tinged with subtle notes of Kenyan. It only took a moment longer to respond because I was simply in awe at the affluence of the neighborhood.

Moments later, we came to a stop in front of a beautifully eclectic skyscraper. I looked up at the multi-floor building and it rivaled any of the luxury condos in Atlanta. The curved glass and metal facade juxtaposed with geometric angles of glass and steel outer buildings, showed off architectural artistry. *Impressive.*

Okiyo climbed effortlessly out of the SUV, coming around to open my door before I could so much as reach for my carryon. He dexterously reached over me to grab the strap of the bag, handing it off to a porter who'd already retrieved my small suitcase from the back and had already moved to vanish into the glass doors of the lobby. Okiyo placed a firm hand on my elbow and assisted me out of the vehicle with no preamble. *If he wasn't so dark and evasive, I could get used to this. Handsome and a gentleman. Well gentleman was probably a stretch, He was efficient as hell though.*

My elbow still in his hand, Okiyo guided me up the steps from the curb, through the automatic doors to the welcome desk of the opulent lobby. The waiting concierge flashed a gleaming white smile, reaching out a hand, and without introduction she welcomed, "Ms. Bainswright, we've been waiting for you."

"Oh." I was surprised by the personal greeting by name. I offered my hand, matching her warmth and looking for her name tag. "Please call me Andra, Layla. Such a beautiful name." I said before studying my surroundings of the lobby further.

Everything, from the beautiful glass encased concierges' desk, to the beautiful blue marbling of the floors, and the floor-to-ceiling iridescent mosaic tile on the walls were breathtaking.

"This place is amazing, too," I gushed.

Layla smiled at both compliments and continued with the check-in process. Not before I noticed her appreciative gaze at Okiyo, who may as well have been on guard at the *Tomb of the Unknown Soldier* he was so utterly disinterested. So buttoned up and closed off that I'd almost forgotten he was there until I noticed the armed security guards flanking the desk. Okiyo, was talking to one of them in hushed tones as I continued chatting with Layla, the concierge who'd just handed me the keys for the condo I'd be staying in and explaining how the turnstiles to access the elevators up to the living area worked.

She paused briefly, eyes fluttering, as Okiyo walked up to the desk. She tried to hide the seductive gleam in her eye before quickly masking it before looking back at me. "You are all set. Also, the studio has delivered your wardrobe and other necessities. You will find them already hanging and organized in the closet. I oversaw that myself and if you have any problems with the way things are laid out please do let me know."

She leaned in, eyes swiping from me to Okiyo then back to me, "Mr. Bamdi, here, called and said you may be starving after such a long flight so I had the kitchen make you a charcuterie board to snack on. Also, your favorite wine, Apothic Red, no?"

"Ummm, yes," I stammered, shocked at how my every need had been anticipated.

"Great. A bottle is already chilling in the refrigerator for you."

This time, speaking to Okiyo and openly flirting with him now, she winked. "She's all set."

He nodded, a low chuckle in his throat as if very familiar with her brand of flirtatiousness. He then turned to me. This time, extending his hand. I tentatively grabbed it and he pulled mine to his lips again to kiss the back of it.

He straightened, releasing me, before stating, "Ms. Bainswright, the studio would like for you to take tomorrow to settle into your accommodations. Oh," He paused, then reached into the breast pocket of his jacket, pulling out an iPhone, handing it to me. "You are probably aware by now that your American cell phone is roaming. This cell phone is already set up for you on the Safari link network. My number is the only number programmed in it. If you need anything please do not hesitate to call. I expect you will be hungry in the morning. There is an onsite restaurant but it doesn't open until lunch. Dial me when you're hungry or if you'd like to explore the city."

I nodded in understanding of his instructions. He placed the phone in my hand, curtly bowing his head at both me and the receptionist before turning on his heel towards the exit to the waiting vehicle outside. We both watched him walk away. Both enjoying the view.

I used the key to unlock the door, excited to see if the condo was decked out as well as the lobby. I took the first step into the foyer and the lights came on automatically. I took more steps beyond and with each, more lights came on to illuminate my way. Each room I entered; I was presented with more luxury, more automation, more... more. It all unfolded before me.

The living room had turquoise wingback chairs and a stylish white sofa arranged in front of a wall of windows, curved in the same shape of the building's façade. The view of the city through the window wall was spectacular.

The nightlife of the city twinkled like radiant stars below. On the drive in, I noticed several small party spots, restaurants, and boutiques. And though it was after midnight, the city still bustled. I was going to have fun exploring.

There were two bedrooms in the condo. The main had an ensuite bathroom decked in the same mosaic tile of the lobby. There was a white marble sink with a deep basin and flat touch-controlled knobs that controlled the water. An expensive mirror lined the wall behind the double vanity sink. I shuddered at the face that stared back at me. The wariness of the trip was etched into my eyes. The little makeup I'd worn on the trip was all but gone by now. Damn, no wonder Jason Statham's black body double hadn't given me a second glance.

Shrugging, I left the bathroom opting to explore the closet tomorrow. I was exhausted. I'd call Kobe first thing in the morning. I retrieved my toiletry bag from my luggage that had been placed at the foot of the bed. Not moments after showering, I was in bed fast asleep.

Chapter 9 - Kobe

♥

"AHH," I MOANED. HEAD lolling back into the cushions of my couch.

Shay was doing that pepper grinding thing that she did with both hands wrapped around the base of my dick. The sound of her slurping and gagging on the head should have had my toes curling, but to be honest, I wasn't that into it. Her head game was fire. Felt good as fuck, even. I just wasn't that into her.

I was almost relieved to hear the incoming FaceTime alert on my phone. But when I looked and saw the call was from an unknown number. I ignored it. Three seconds later when I was throwing my head back moaning, my phone alerted again, this time vibrating in my palm.

I peeked at the screen, not wanting to interrupt Shay from handling her business. It was a text from the same unknown number now coming through. My curiosity over the phone alert outweighed what Shay was doing. I clicked to open the message. I sat up quickly, pulling my dick from Shay's lips. It was Andra.

Andra: It's me, nigga. stop screening your calls. Studio gave me an iPhone (head exploding emoji). About to Facetime you back.

Me: oh shit! You done came up! Aight. Bet. Call me back.

Within seconds the distinctive alert came through. This time I answered. Not daring to look down at Shay, whose eyes I could feel burning into me.

Nonplussed I'm sure. She sucked her teeth. Loud.

"Thought I told yo' pecan tan ass to call me as soon as you landed?" I answered the phone. Glad to finally hear from Andra.

"Sorry, babe. I meant to. But as soon as I landed and got my bags, this black Jason Statham looking transportation liaison," she said holding up a hand signing air quotes when she said, 'transportation liaison', "Scooped me up from the airport before I could call. And honestly by the time I got to the roomy condo," she stated, eyes gleaming with excitement, "I was too tired to do anything other than wash my ass and get under the covers."

"It's all good. I'm just glad you made it OK. And I see you big balling with the iPhone now!"

"Right!" Andra exclaimed, eyes big and full of animation, "Yo, when I say they spared no expense with this trip, Kobe. Bruh. This iPhone ain't even the half." She flipped the camera around, giving me a panoramic view of a wall. "Wait until you see this baller ass apartment!"

"What are you waiting on? Let me see it," I said, matching her excitement, laughing when she realized she wasn't showing me anything.

"First off, let me show you this living room and this damn view. Honey," she drug out the syllables then snapped her fingers for emphasis, "There is a whole curved wall of glass! I have an all-glass fucking wall, Kobe! Do you see this?" she said, spinning around so I could see the curved wall of glass and the rest of the space which was decked out in beautiful furnishings.

"Damn, Andra, a white couch? Ain't no kids ever been up in there!" I laughed, impressed at the set up.

I felt, rather heard, Shay snatch away from me. She stalked past me to the kitchen to snatch open the refrigerator to just stand there staring into it looking pissed. Of course, her ass walked right in the line of sight of my camera.

Seeing that I had company, Andra rolled her eyes at me on screen. "Oomph," she said, sucking her teeth, "Why didn't you tell me you had company?"

Thank God I had my earpiece in and Shay couldn't hear the other half of the conversation. I looked back behind me before responding to Andra and just as I knew she would, Shay was shooting daggers across the kitchen at me with her eyes. I looked back at the phone at an irritated Andra. "Yeah Shay came over. We kickin' it." I made sure to say it out loud.

"Were kicking it," I heard Shay mumble under her breath behind me. I was about to get an earful from her as soon as I hung up the phone. She continued to mumble under her breath as I wrapped up my call with Andra. "Baby, *gyul*, I'm about to go."

Andra pursed her lips and shook her head at me.

I really wasn't in the mood to deal with Shay's mouth tonight, but it was rude of me to answer the call in the middle of what she was doing. In my defense, my anxiety was up a little waiting on Andra to call. I needed to know she was ok.

"Kobe, one more thing I want to show you and then I'm going to let you get back to your lil' company," Andra said, back to being excited. Quickly walking over to a corner of the guest bedroom. "They even have a Peloton in here. So, guess what my nigga?"

"What's that, Baby, *gyul*?"

"We can finally use the video chat feature when we work out!"

"Yo. That's what's up. And now that I've officially resigned as head chef at Jah, I can set my workouts around yours. What time is it over there anyway?"

"It's just after 7:00 AM here. I think I'm 8 hours ahead of you. So that makes it..." She paused, trying to count back the hours.

"Just after 11 PM. With your non counting ass." I laughed.

"Oh, hush up." She giggled. "It's late there. Get back to your... company. I'm about to get dressed up in my new clothes, courtesy of the studio, and call up my 'transportation liaison'," she said it again with air quotes, tossing her braids over her shoulder in pure Andra style. I was going to have to get her to explain the transportation liaison thing. Later. Right now, I needed to deal with the wrath of Shay.

"Miss you already, Anj. I'm going to hold you to those workouts. I'll be up at the ass crack of dawn in the morning to meet with the studio execs about the restaurant. I know you like to work out in the evening and shit so let's put that Peloton to work," I stated. "I'll be online around 4:00AM. And just so you know, that's 8:00 PM for your non counting ass."

"Umm...No. That math ain't mathing. 4:00 AM for you will be noon for me. Who can't count now?" We both laughed at that.

"Oh, wait," I rushed to stop her from hanging up and still stalling, "I think we should do a slow drip campaign to let our followers know about the tv show and restaurant."

"Yeah, I agree. Don't want to spring it all on them at once. Plus we can create some good buzz around it with some strategic messaging." She paused, thinking for a minute. "You know, since you are going to have to get used to managing our socials for a minute, come up with something catchy."

I was thinking about ideas for Gastrafrique when we hung up the call. Explains why I was caught off guard when Shay rounded on my ass as soon as I put my phone down.

"You ain't bout to sit up here and play in my face, Kobe. Talking about you and that bitch ain't fucking!"

Here we go. Same argument, different day.

"Girl what the hell are you talking about? For the last time, Andra is my best friend and business partner," I said calmly. "We ain't never fucked. Never even kissed." I couldn't help but think about how we almost kissed yesterday but wouldn't tell Shay that. "Not when we were 13. Not when we were 23. Not when we were 33. And we ain't fucking now."

"Yeah, yeah," she said pushing past me towards my bedroom, "Save the bullshit for the next bitch. Ain't no man 'bout to answer no phone while he getting his dick sucked for a bitch he ain't fucking!"

Damn she had a point. Except, me and Andra were just friends.. Before I could grab her ass to stop her from leaving, Crazy-Balls met her at the door of my bedroom growling. So instead of grabbing Shay to coax her into staying, I had to calm my nearly hundred-pound Mastiff down. It was at that moment that I realized that it probably would be best if Shay did leave. We'd only been kicking it for about a month. Andra disliked her on site, saying Shay was a bit too ghetto for me and it wasn't going to work out.

But like the sucker trying to super save. I tried to make that square peg fit into this round hole.

Shay was cool people. Was fine as frog hairs, too. But she didn't have any drive about her. And apparently, Andra knew me better than I knew myself, because as she'd called it, I was already bored with Shay. Just didn't want to hurt her feelings. I needed a woman with substance. Shay wasn't it.

Two years older than me, she stayed in the club and at the hookah spots across Atlanta More than I did in my early 20s. The fact that neither my best friend, nor my dog liked her should have been telling.

They say babies and dogs know good people when they see them. And Balls didn't see any good in this one. Best to let her go. She picked up her bag and dropped a few f-bombs at me on her way to the door, followed by my 100-pound black mastiff and this 200-pound black man, closing it behind her for the last time.

I wasn't quite sleepy yet so I decided to sit down and work on some content for Gastrafrique. We chose not to announce it yet, rather build some suspense to drive up engagement. So that's what I did. I created a cryptic post that was a picture of a wall feature that I really wanted to do inside the waiting area of the restaurant once it was built out. The only words across the picture were 'Good News!'

Andra was going to post the next post and it would have a similar background picture but in the same fancy font. The only text would be 'Got.' The third and last post in the small campaign would be another picture, keeping the same theme as the first two, a simple image of my hand whipping up something over a high flame in a kitchen, with only the word 'We've.' The post would go in backwards back-to-back but whenever someone went to the Gastrafrique profile page, they would see the message fully spelled out, 'we've got good news!' And the buzz would be generated.

Chapter 10 – Andra

♥

IT WAS HALF PAST 9 in the morning, when I finished getting dressed in the cute denim culotte jumpsuit, courtesy of the studio. I was impressed at how well they got my style. I scavenged through the wide assortment of accessories and shoes also curated just for me, settling for gold tennis shoes, a gazillion gold bangles on both wrists and a small gold YSL crossbody to pull it all together. Everything fit me to a 'T.'

I was going for a chill vibe hoping to explore the city in the daytime. I made light work of my makeup and hair and was ready to hit the door as soon as I pulled my braids into a high ponytail.

Time to call my ride.

He'd said his number was the only one programmed into my new phone. Sure enough, the singular contact read, Okiyo Bamdi. I let the syllables roll over my tongue as I said them aloud. Laughing at myself as I mimicked his accent. I pressed the button to connect the call.

"Ms. Bainswright," he answered. "I presume you are in need of a car."

"You presume right, Mr. Bamdi. Or should I call you Okiyo?"

"Mr. Bamdi is fine. I will be up to retrieve you in five minutes." Click.

Lord have mercy. The cool he had going on last night was straight kiddie pool compared to the deep freeze he was serving up today. And just as he'd stated over the phone, he was outside my door, precisely five minutes later.

I grabbed my bag and opened the door. Almost wanted to go back and change when I saw what the Kenyan James Bond was wearing. He was decked out in an impeccably fitted navy suit, complete with a crisp collar, straight tie, vest and pocket square. Shit. I was underdressed next to him. Changing was not an option after he held out a stiff elbow and commanded, "Come with me."

I did. Grabbed the offered arm, feeling the flex of his bicep as I held on. If not for his staunch professionalism, my panties might have melted.

Once I safely tucked into the backseat of the same SUV from last night, he took his seat beside me. Once settled he asked, "Any thoughts on what you would like to do today, Ms. Bainswright?"

Over him and ready to enjoy the outing, I answered quickly, "Yes. I'd like to eat an authentic Kenyan lunch. I've heard that Nairobi Street Kitchen is a nice spot."

Before I could finish my sentence, a chuckle escaped from Deke, the driver, before he quickly recovered. Okiyo all but rolled his eyes at my suggestion before calmly saying, "Authentic hardly has a place in the same sentence with Nairobi Street Kitchen." A smile played around the perimeter of his lips, softening his austere words a bit, before he continued. "Mama Oliech's, Deke." Another command. He sat back in his seat, occupying himself with his phone, paying me no more mind. Without question Deke headed to Mama Oliech's.

I didn't know whether to be offended or amused with this man taking my eating choices into his own hands. If this shit was nasty, I was going to savor letting him know just how tasteless he was.

Twenty minutes later, we pulled into a gravel courtyard. Patrons of various types, businessmen and women in suits, some in athletic gear fresh off a morning workout, and families with kids were eating outside seated around the courtyard.

The atmosphere at Mama Oliech's was casual and was authentic Kenyan cuisine. From the family style dining complete with shared dishes in the centers of the table. To the meats on the far side of the courtyard being roasted over an open flame. The melded scent of a variety of spices; turmeric, coriander, and cumin wafted through the air. This was as authentic as it got.

Everyone was chatting, laughing, and enjoying good food. We exited the vehicle and were met in the center of the courtyard by a waiter. He immediately showed us to a table, then guided our attention to an outdoor spicket for us to wash our hands.

I looked up at the sound of Okiyo chuckling as he watched me stare at the menu in confusion. It may as well have been upside down because I couldn't read a word of it because it was fully in Swahili.

And to think, I'd studied the language on and off for years, and got here to understand only a few words. My ability to read and speak the language hit different outside of the *Babble* app.

He graciously leaned in and began explaining some of the options on the menu. Thankful for the assistance, I opted for the Ugali, a thick white cornmeal mush resembling fufu and whole tilapia. It came complete with thinly shredded greens and a spicy red sauce that I ended up putting over everything.

Really, I thought as I proceeded to eat my self silly, while Okiyo let his hair down just enough to enjoy a cup of coffee.

Satisfied that I'd eaten my fill, he paid the tab and ushered me to the waiting vehicle as if I were a superstar. To be honest, I could get used to this shit.

When asked what I'd like to do next. My mind drew a blank. I'd eaten so much that all I really wanted to do was go take a nap. But the way my hips were set up, I needed to walk off some of this food. "Outside of finding great food, I didn't have a specific thing in mind to do. Thought we could just explore," I said, sitting back heavily in the seat, hands rested over my slightly extended belly. "Whatever we do, I need to walk some of this food off."

"Would you like to peruse the shops at the Sarit Centre?" He asked aloofly. I'm sure he assumed that every woman would be down to go to the mall and shop. In my case, he was right, but I wasn't on that right now. I had a whole closet of new clothes at the condo. All courtesy of the Food Network and some unknown benefactor.

"I was thinking something a little bit more adventurous and maybe outside." To that, he lifted an eyebrow, nodding his head ever so slightly in agreement. Again, tossing an order over the driver's seat, "Giraffe Manor, Deke." Deke nodded and we were off.

My breath hitched when I heard the location.

"I could fucking kiss you," I squealed, delighted about where we were going. Giraffe Manor was only one of the most Instagrammed properties in the world! I'd read about the exclusive boutique hotel. It was home to the resident herd of Rothschild's giraffes who would visit the historic 1930's manor in the morning and evening in hopes of a treat. I'd seen many travel photos on Instagram of the long-necked creatures, poking their heads in windows of the private rooms, licking their tongues at guests, coaxing them to feed them.

"A kiss won't be necessary, Ms. Bainswright." A fleeting smile breaking through his cool veneer.

"You know I don't really mean to kiss you," I smacked, "I mean, I've read about this place. It's one of mine and Kobe's bucket list items!"

"Kobe?" he lifted a brow, then recognition dawned. "Oh yes, your lover in the states."

"Hunh?" I sputtered, "Kobe is not my lover." I was so quick to rebut his statement that it didn't immediately occur to me to ask why he'd drawn that conclusion in the first place., "Kobee's my best friend and business partner," I chose to ignore his barely perceptible snort, continuing, "Wait, how do you know about Kobe, anyway? Better yet how are you going to get us into Giraffe Manor? I heard the waiting list was months long with a booked stay?"

"I do my research and I have my ways, Ms. Bainswright." And just like that, the book of Okiyo Bamdi closed again. *This C.I.A nigga...* I was too excited about our destination to press him further and thoroughly enjoyed the outing. The Manor was something straight out of a dream, even with Okiyo's stiff presence as my chaperone.

Unsurprisingly, the real stars of the show were the giraffes. They gave everything I needed them to give when I handed Okiyo my phone and asked him to film me with them. They'd stretched their long, graceful necks to peek into the window, their large, curious eyes looking for treats.

I'd never been so close to a giraffe. The ones at Zoo Atlanta wouldn't give you the time of day. The lashes of these beautiful beasts were like little fans, fluttering as they chewed. I fed them, laughed with them, even got slobbery giraffe kisses.

I could have sworn I caught Okiyo cracking a smile once or twice. Maybe it was the magic of the manor, or maybe it was the sight of me, wide-eyed and giggling like a child. Either way, he managed to be good company.

By the time I made it back to my condo in the Westlands, I only had 10 minutes to meet Kobe on the Peloton for our pre-planned Tabata Ride with the infamous Alex Toussant. I'd messaged him while out with Okiyo that we'd have to do the later ride. I couldn't wait to tell him about Giraffe Manor. He was going to be so jealous.

I was fully dressed in Ivy Park running tights and a sports bra in 5 minutes flat. I logged into my account on the new Peloton, not having enough time to adjust the seat and handlebars to my height before clicking on the live class that was about to start. The current set up would have to do for now. I joined just as Alex Toussant's voice came through the speaker on the screen:

"What's going on Peloton! My name is Alex Toussant. Welcome to our 30-minute Future ride, baby! One of the greatest rappers, in all honesty, of the generation! While I have you here with us today, quick rundown on that tablet. The left side of the screen is your speed. When I call it, you match it... Let's go!"

I scrolled and found Kobe in the list of cyclists in the class and clicked the video chat button, turning his volume up and Alex's voice down.

"Wow!" I said, impressed as Kobe's face came into view in the upper left corner of the screen attached to the sleek cycle. "This video is clear as shit!"

"Damn. It really is," he nodded his head in agreement taking me in through the video display offering me a sly smile.. "You know this is an Alex Toussaint class right? I'm about to watch all that makeup melt off your face!"

I laughed at his silliness. He always got onto me about not taking the time to wash off my makeup before going to the gym. Today he was right. I didn't have time and was looking forward to jumping on this live ride.

"You are so right," I grimaced as soon as the instructor, known for his heart pounding in your face rides, started yelling the 1,2,1,2 count to get everyone moving out the gate at an 80 to 100 cadence. My face immediately started to heat up.

"Alex is about to break our asses off and my dumb ass is about to record some footage for our page." I'd had the sense to connect my mobile tripod to the handlebar of the bike. Everything was content in our world.

"Good idea. Eventually, the followers will know you're in Kenya. It will make sense to them why we're using this new video feature and posting about it."

We were about 5 minutes into the thirty-minute ride and I began telling Kobe all about my day and experience at Giraffe Manor. I could see his eyes narrow a bit. I knew he'd feel some kind of way about me going. We'd talked about it so many times. Didn't last long as he genuinely laughed out loud at some of the shenanigans of the giraffes I told him about. Eventually the ride became so intense that we ceased talking so we could power through the torture of the AT ride.

"I'm glad you got to enjoy it and have some down time before filming starts. Y'all start soon right?" he said towards the end of the class during the cooldown.

"Yep. Start filming. Two days," I huffed, still fighting to catch my breath. "You're meeting with the realtor today to look for the restaurant space, right?"

"Yep. Matter of fact, about to shower and head out as soon as we're done and I get off this bike," He said.

The class ended almost as soon as Kobe finished his last statement. You'd think that the good time I had today at the manor and chopping it up with Kobe over a full out aerobic workout, paired with jet lag, I'd be exhausted. I was exactly the opposite. I was pumped.

" Let me know if you see some good properties." I said as he toweled off, "This was fun. We gotta do it again later in the week." I said, toeing out of my riding cleats too.

"Let's do it," He said, swiping the drenched towel over his face. "Let's keep using the video. Almost felt like you were right here."

Because I was so wired, I decided to stretch so that my muscles wouldn't start cramping, then jump on another ride on the Peloton to burn off some of this extra energy.

Fifteen minutes later, I was strapped back into my cycling shoes on the bike. I only had to touch the screen to bring the monitor back to life. It was then that I realized that neither Kobe nor I had ended the video chat feature and I had a full view of his dining room clear into the adjacent kitchen.

I made a mental note to let him know that the video didn't automatically end at the end of a class, we'd have to... Whoa!

Before I could finish the thought, Kobe rounded the corner from his bedroom straight into the kitchen, butt-assed naked. And his dick... Gawt-damn. That monster led the way to the refrigerator where he began pulling out the makings for his customary smoothie.

Finally released from the chokehold he had me in, I wrestled to end the chat before the saliva that had pooled at the corner of my mouth dribbled down my chin. My desire to burn off more energy is all but forgotten. A cold shower would suffice.

Chapter 11 – Andra

♥

H E MOVED CLOSER. FINALLY leaning in for a passionate kiss. I felt like I'd been waiting a lifetime for his lips to touch mine. I lit on fire as soon as the soft satin of his lips met my hungry uncontrollable desire. His hands explored my curves with wild intensity. My heart raced, threatening to open my chest. His touch burned like nothing I'd experienced before - it both scared and excited me at the same time.

We moved closer still as if guided by some unknown force, until we finally reached a table in the back of the room. He lifted me. The cool edge under my ass added to the blissful sensations. Every part of me was radiating pleasure as our bodies melded.

The contrast of his dark hands against the molten gold of my thighs as he wrenched them apart took me even higher.

It took only a second for him to have me open to him, filling the space between us with his monstrous dick leveled at my slick wetness. My soul left my body. I hovered over us watching, feeling his full erection slowly inch into me. I gripped the edge of the steel prep table.

"Ahh," I cried. He inched deeper.

The dim candlelight cast a seductive glow over the room, while the smell of spices filled the air. The heady aroma of cinnamon, cardamom, nutmeg, invaded my senses. Tickling my nose, as his chest hairs tickled my nipples.

He inched a little deeper. I moaned again. This time louder as my walls spasmed around his fullness. The tightness he created in my pussy had me wanting to beg him - fuck me already.

He. Went. Slower. The agony of wanting him buried deep in me threatened to drive me insane.

Sensing my frenzy, he whispered, "I've waited my entire life for this, baby. Just let me savor this moment."

I whimpered, acquiescing in his arms. I wrapped my legs around his waist and an arm around his neck, leaning back pulling him into me on the table. He put his soft lips on mine, letting them linger as though etching their taste and feel to memory.

His body shuttered from the slow torture he was rendering to me and to himself. Another eternity passed before he lifted his head. His smoldering gaze pierced me, while his hips suspended over mine. Then without warning, he let out a guttural cry as he bit into the soft flesh of my shoulder, ramming his perfectly hard dick into my...

I woke up with a start! Entire body flushed. My own wetness lubricating my thighs. I was suddenly embarrassed at the realization that I was having an intimate dream about Kobe. *What the fuck!*

A flashback of his dick invaded my thoughts as I lay tangled in the sheets, tugging them over my head as if they would block out the image. I groaned as flashbacks of our naked bodies twisting around each other - in the kitchen of Jah, came flooding back.

I'd visited Kobe enough times over the years to know every detail of that place. And in my dream we were about to fuck where somebodies' food would be plated.

I dragged myself out of bed already feeling off my game. "Ugh," I groaned forcing myself to start getting dressed. Today was the first day of shooting. One thing I knew for sure was that I was going to have to sort out why in the holy hell that dream had my ass getting wet all over again just thinking of him.

As soon as that stupid little clapper thing clapped and the director said action, I was a nervous wreck. This was nothing like filming myself – or food, or the interior of a restaurant, on my phone. It was ten times worse than the first time Kobe and I went live on IG.

I had spent days preparing for the first day of shooting. The segment featured me cooking one of the recipes Kobe and I had concocted for Gastrafrique. It was our take on Jollof Rice fused with Louisiana style dirty rice. I'd made this countless times before. But made a clumsy mess of it today on camera.

I was overwhelmed at first by the hustle and bustle of the cast and crew running here and there, barking orders to set up for the shoot. I began sweating when I realized I didn't have Kobe by my side either laughing at my silliness or being my sous-chef. My pussy spasming at the sheer thought of him, made matters worse.

We were in the middle of the eighth take. The director had already shouted action and everyone around me seemed to freeze, intent on watching me plate the food I'd just prepared. Something so simple as plating food, Something I'd watched Kobe do a million times. And today of all days, as I thought of how he would plate the food to perfection, all I could seem to conjure were his hands gliding gracefully over the rim of the plate, touching it...ever so tenderly.

Ugh... I groaned inwardly. While everyone on set had their eyes on me, I was stuck in a daydream, thoughts of his tall muscular frame bent over caressing a got-damn plate. \

"Cut!" The director's shout echoed across the set.

Fuck. She was on her way over to me, and everyone else started scampering around to reset for the next take. All I could feel was the buzz of my nerves that I was going to have to shake. God, please let me make it through this next take.

"Andra, take five." Kayla, the director said over the counter I was standing behind.. "You're doing fine. The nerves are normal," she said.

I rolled my eyes to the sky, hands clasped behind my head after releasing the white-knuckled grip on the countertop. I nodded before blowing air forcefully out of my puckered lips, a breathing trick for nerves I'd learned from somewhere.

Seeing the defeat in my face, she added, "This is your first day. Don't beat yourself up too much. You'll get it on the next shot."

"I hope so," I said as I walked to get some water from the break room.

The days of shooting dragged on and I could feel my self-confidence steadily diminishing. I had to humbly admit to myself that I sucked at scripted acting. I couldn't blame that on the fucked-up dream I'd had about my best friend either. But... I was committed to this show being a success, so I dug in my heels and did my best each time. I was able to stop thinking about the dream with Kobe, but still wasn't ready to talk to him for fear I'd act awkward trying to talk around that long, thick black elephant trunk that would be in the room, just beneath the waistline of his pants.

Today we were on set filming the last few takes of the in-studio portion of a segment on wine. I was interviewing Mbugua Ngugi, the purveyor of Leleshwa, Kenya's premier winery. I was seated across from him and the interview started out like previous days but I trudged through.

Our chat was a lively back-and-forth, punctuated with tales of wine creation and delectable pairings. With every sip of the wines he served, particularly the semi-sweet Rose with its lively notes, my tension began to fade. It was like the wine was a lullaby, soothing my jitters and bringing forth the confident, charismatic me.

Mbugua, with his effortless charm, was like a well-timed compliment. I didn't desire him romantically or anything, but his attention was like a spotlight I was only too ready to bask in. It eased me, loosened me up, and I found myself sinking into the moment, flirting right back and responding to the playful banter.

The cameras hummed in the background, capturing the evolution. A little loose off the wine, all but forgot the scripted words, replaced them with raw authenticity. I was lost in the rhythm of the conversation, the shared stories of East African winemaking.

Suddenly, a "Cut!" resonated through the studio. Instinctively, my heart clenched. That word was usually a harbinger of my mistakes, a call for retakes. I glanced at Kayla, steeling myself for the critique.

Instead, she was all smiles. "Great job, Andra! You nailed it."

Surprise hit me like a flashbulb. *I'd nailed it? In one take?* That realization swept over me, soon followed by a surge of satisfaction. I had stepped into the moment, had been as charismatic and natural as I knew I was capable of being.

It felt damn fantastic.

Mr. Ngugi was preparing to leave when Kayla had been called away by the producer to speak with a man I didn't recognize in the back of the studio. Reaching out his hand, he said, "I usually don't do interviews, but I'm glad I did. I hope that you can join me in Naivasha at the winery for a real tour."

"That would be great. My filming schedule is tight, but maybe I can make it out," I fluttered my lashes at him, still on a high from the success of the segment we'd just finished recording.

"I will personally give you a tour," He winked.

It really was too bad he wasn't my type, else, I'd be on my way to free wine for life tonight.

No sooner than he was gone, Kayla sidled back up. I was bracing for the reprimand for going off script. She hadn't mentioned it a few moments ago. Maybe she was waiting for Mr. Ngugi to leave so I wouldn't be totally embarrassed.

The man she'd been speaking to was distinguished. I noticed him immediately when he entered the set during the shoot. I was engrossed in the interview with Mr. Ngugi, but this man had a presence that couldn't be missed. Whoever he was, he must have held some weight around the crew because their energy shifted. They were popping taller; Working harder. *Lord, I went off script in front of a studio exec. He'd probably given the order for Kayla to axe my ass.*

"Andra, I couldn't help but notice that you ditched the script and all the preplanned questions during the interview."

"I did," I said, wringing my hands, knowing I'd fucked up. "They just didn't feel right," I started, "I'm sorry. It won't happ—"

She cut me off. "No, no. It worked. You killed that shit."

"So I'm not getting fired?" I smiled nervously.

She chuckled, shaking her head at me thoughtfully. "I think we have been going about this all wrong. You know the subject matter of each segment and you've clearly researched each guest. Hell you know more about some of the guests than I do and I'm from Kenya," Kayla gave a self-deprecating laugh. "We've been trying to force you into a package that you just don't fit. From here on out, fuck the script! You're a natural and your authenticity really showed through today."

I stood there stunned. She giggled. A strange sight because she was usually a beast on set. All business and yelling orders at everyone. This was the first time I'd seen her smile.

"And... we just got the green light to go out into the field early to start recording the onsite segments. We leave in two days to go out to the Maasai Mara for a cultural segment."

"The Maasai Mara? That's not one of the segments on the list." I was perplexed. I knew the schedule, the guests, and the location shoots like the back of my hand. The Maasai Mara wasn't on it.

"Well, dear, It is now. You did such a thorough job of interviewing the last guest, that we are replacing the onsite at his winery with this new segment. Of course, we'll send a crew out to the winery to get some footage, but none that you'd need to be in. That's reality tv, dear. Things change quickly. We leave tomorrow. And it will be totally unscripted. So bring your A-game!"

"Uhhh... but. How..?" She left me stammering.

"You got this!" She yelled over her shoulder making her way to share the change in schedule with the rest of the crew.

As an afterthought, she stopped. She turned back to me. "Pack comfortable stuff. This is more Ivy Park than YSL. Long sleeves, nothing tight. Tennis shoes. Absolutely no heels!" She stressed, looking me up and down and twisting her lips at the bodycon dress and 4-inch heels I had on today. "It'll be hot. And we'll be at a camp out in the bush." She was back to giving orders.

Chapter 12 –Kobe

♥

I PULLED MY RANGE Rover into a parking space right in front of the newly constructed commercial property in the highly sought after Parque Place, a new live, play, work development in the heart of Atlanta. I strained my neck to see through my windshield up at the building to see 1679 etched into its side. This was the fifth property my realtor had shown me today and my patience was wearing thin. None of them seemed to fit what I envisioned for the Gastrafrique restaurant.

What I wanted was something special: an impressive bar area; a spacious waiting area; and a dining room ,befitting Michelin-star standards, with modern decor inspired by both mine and Andra's African roots. None of the first few places gave anything near what I was looking for. They looked more like Bob's Diner than five-star dining. Still, even though I wasn't expecting much from building 1679, I had committed to seeing all five locations.

As Isadora and I stepped out of the car and towards the building where we were greeted by the building manager, she threw a comment over her shoulder, "Saved the best for last Mr. Abara." Her beaming smile suggested she was keeping a secret from me; so, with an open mind, I opened the door and gestured for her to enter ahead of me in anticipation of what extraordinary sights lay before us inside this new space.

As soon as I stepped through the front door of 1679, I could tell it was exactly what I was looking for - and Isadora's comment suddenly made sense. Even though nothing had been built out yet, I could already imagine it in my mind. The waiting area just within the doorway was modern and inviting, with low seating and artwork on the walls. Even the intake hostess desk seemed to stand out before me.

As I moved past Isadora further into the open space, it felt like my vision for Gastrafrique exploded in living color. With each step forward, I could visualize where the bar would be situated, envisioning dark colors and a sexy atmosphere that resonated with the alluring appeal of Mother Africa.

The dark colors and cool vibe were already clear in my mind - lo-fi hip hop and Afrobeats playing in the background as patrons dined at precisely lit tables; women out for a Friday night looking for a good time with their friends gathering in one corner; men on a Wednesday night sitting at the bar, collars unbuttoned, ties relaxed as they enjoyed their drink of choice.

My first inclination was to whip out my phone and Facetime Andra. She had to see this place. It just rang. She hadn't answered my calls in a couple of days. I blew it off, figuring she was busy filming. Pictures would have to suffice. I'd Airdrop them to her later.

"Isadora, my girl," I say, turning to face her. "Picture this - a sleek bar, smooth bartenders doing their thing. It's like watching a performance - they're creating something magical right before your eyes."

Isadora nods, her eyes lighting up with excitement. "Adding some African, West African, and Kenyan design elements are sure to make the space unique," she says, her notebook at the ready, taking notes for the design team. I nod in agreement, my mind already racing with possibilities.

"Bright colors, bold patterns, woven textures," I say. "And maybe we could find some traditional African art pieces to display."

Isadora continues to scribble in her notepad, her brow furrowed with concentration. "I like it," she says. "It'll give the space a really cool vibe."

I grin, feeling a sense of satisfaction. This is gonna be something special - I can feel it. And then there's the feature wall.

"I've got an idea for the feature wall," I say, my voice dropping to a whisper. "It's gonna blow Andra's mind when she sees it."

Isadora looks at me curiously. "What do you have in mind?" she asks.

I smiled, feeling a sense of excitement building inside of me. "I'm thinking of beads," I say. "A big, bold wall made of beads, just like the ones Andra always wears. It'll be a tribute to her and a way to make the space truly capture her essence."

Isadora's eyes narrow, "Did you mean to say, Gastrafrique's essence?"

"Hunh?" I take in her question.

"You said, take in her essence. As in Andra's? I thought you meant Gastrafrique's essence is all. A cohesive look for Gastrafrique."

"Oh yeah," I said to her, shaking my head. I was thinking about Andra but I didn't need to let Isadora know that.

When Andra saw the feature wall I truly wanted to dedicate to her, she's going to be blown away.

"So..." Isadora said, blowing off the brief awkward moment, "As you can see, this space is brand new construction - no business has ever been here before. Parque Place is the hottest mixed-use space in town and according to market research, the foot traffic is unbeatable. However, I must caution you that the lease amount for this space is threefold what we've seen elsewhere."

"This is it," I looked at her, unable to contain my excitement. "This is Gastrafrique. We'll take it," I declared without hesitation. The studio was serious about sparing no expense and I was determined to make our dream a reality. As long as I had full creative control, me and the interior designer would transform this place into something truly special.

"Let's get the paperwork drawn up and sent over so we can review it, get it signed, and sent back right away. I want to make sure this space is firmly secured before anyone has a chance to beat us to it." I provided her with my email address as well as the executive team addresses that would be signing off on the transaction.

I left the restaurant and headed straight over to headquarters, anticipating a battle to be waged for my choice of the pricier Parque Place location for Gastrafrique. Much to my surprise, there was zero resistance – in fact, they practically pushed me out the door so I could get started on the buildout. They did provide a list of contractors who specialized in high-end restaurant build outs as well as an interior designer who was an expert in trendy Atlanta eateries.

I asked for two additional designers that I could personally vet, because there was no way I wanted Gastrafrique blending in with all the other run-of-the-mill lounges, restaurants, and "hot spots" that had recently popped up across town.

I looked down at my phone for the umpteenth time to see if Andra had tried to call me back. Maybe I'd missed her call while Isadora and I were chopping it up. No missed call. I tried her again, itching to show Andra the space, craving her reaction and hoping it mirrored mine. And although we discussed me taking more of the lead role on content for IG and social media, I still wanted her help— we were a team. My disappointment was starting to set in.

A glance at the time filled me with a little hope in finding out what's been up with her. Our weekly Peloton workout , as we agreed to do to keep us connected despite being miles apart, was in the morning. That brightened my spirits a bit. I was going to have to check her *ahss* about all these unanswered calls and unreturned messages. The fuck, Anj?

I hardly slept the night before; my thoughts teetered between 'is Andra ok?' and 'what the fuck was she doing that she couldn't call me back?'. The latter caused me the most strain. My mind kept going to whether she was laid up with some dude she'd met and didn't think I was important enough to call back. That pissed me off more than I was willing to admit out loud and for reasons less obvious than feeling ignored.

I climb onto the Peloton, hoping to finally get to the bottom of this shit. I was looking forward to using the video feature again. We'd talk, reconnect, do our shared workout and everything would be fine. Except, minutes went by. No Andra.. Her avatar never appeared. A cold wave of disappointment washed over me, yet again.

I pedaled on alone, the physical strain doing little to distract from the void her absence left. It seemed our friendship was taking an unexpected turn, my feelings for Andra becoming a turbulent undercurrent in the sea of confusion. And I was left, wondering what lay ahead for us.

We'd never had a gulf between us like this, physically or emotionally. Andra, filming in Kenya, me hustling in Atlanta—the absence of my confidante stung more than I cared to admit. And it was this absence, this void, that made me reevaluate my feelings for Andra.

Workout finished; I stood face to face with my reflection in the bathroom mirror. The man looking back was anguished "What the fuck Kobe?" I asked myself. "Why are you so pressed about her?" Realization slowly crept through my subconscious becoming strikingly clear. You know why you're pressed. Why was this happening? When did this happen, Kobe?" I questioned out loud to my reflection.

Inwardly, I had to admit, this separation shit, was shifting my feelings for my best friend. The realization left me baffled, a whirlpool of confusion that seemed to consume my thoughts.

Her evasiveness, her silence—it wasn't just puzzling anymore, it downright hurt. Every unreturned call felt like a blow, every missed message like a rejection. Was she deliberately avoiding me?

Chapter 13 – Kobe

♥

ANOTHER WEEK HAD GONE by. No word from Andra except for a short text, apologizing for missing our workout. Filming. That was her excuse. Whatever. I was over it. I guessed eventually we'd catch up. I had to shake this sad shit and get on with the restaurant build out.

I'd selected the designer and threw myself headfirst into working with her and planning out the design concept for Gastrafrique.

Deidre, the interior designer, and I decided to meet up at 1679 to talk through the concept., It was her idea to explore some of the furniture stores, other shops that had recently opened at Parque Place and the surrounding outdoor areas to get a feel for the new location of GAF. I'd taken to calling it that after a couple of conversations with Solita over the last couple of weeks. The nickname had begun to grow on me.

There was the skate park on the property that sparked an idea to incorporate an Afro-futurism theme to the decor. After walking and talking with Deidre, I understood the value of getting a feel for the entire property to see how GAF would be seamlessly integrated inside and out.

She really knew her stuff and sold me on the idea of playing on our social media success and turning every inch of Gastrafrique into an Instagram Story.

As we were walking through the hall of shops back to the restaurant space, I heard someone calling out my name. I turned, surprised that anyone knew I was here today. What I found was a blast from my past. Carmel Dobson. My high school sweetheart—deep brown skin and a face framed by the biggest, fluffiest Afro ever. She was stunning. After the initial shock of seeing her after all these years wore off, I pulled her into a big bear hug.

"Wow, girl," I exclaimed, looking at Carmel with admiration. "I haven't seen you since yours and Andra's graduation from Spelman. How are you?"

Carmel smiled. "Just moved back to the city actually and thought I'd come find some new ingredients for my product line."

"Oh yeah? I see you doing big things," I said with a smirk. "What kind of products are we talking about?"

"I'm trying to do it big like you!" she exclaimed excitedly. "I've been keeping up with what you're doing over on Gastrafrique. Congrats on the 5 million followers."

"Thank you, thank you," I returned. "Yeah, Andra and I have been hustling our asses off for years on IG and it's beginning to pay off for us big time. but tell me about your product line."

"Oh yeah," Carmel nodded excitedly, "I have a line of natural, holistic products for the body." Pride evident in her voice, she continued, "You know, natural organic cleansers, body scrubs, body butters and such -," she paused to dig in her tote, handing me a sample sized something attached to a card with a whimsical logo emblazoned on it. "Here, try this. It's a face cleanser with papaya enzymes in it. Not that you need it or anything, but it brightens dull dry skin. And its edible too." She quickly added.

"Porified," I said reading the name of her product line from the sample. "A play on purified? Clever." I nodded, appreciating the play on words. "And judging by your stunning looks, I can only guess that you're also the model for your brand."

Carmel looked away bashfully, downplaying the compliment. "Yeah. Porified definitely keeps me busy! I started taking a more holistic approach to my own self-care about 5 years ago, and it's been great. Congrats again on the 5 million followers for Gastrafrique, I'm trying to get there! I have to ask. What's this juicy news y'all have?"

"Ahh, you really do follow Gastrafrique," I bellowed, surprised she'd seen the post.

"Ha, doesn't everyone? Y'all have been repping for the motherland and ATL since we were in high school!"

"For 'sho." I said, mystified because she remembered that. I weighed telling her because we hadn't broken the news to our fans yet. Why not? What was she going to do, leak the news to the press or something? "Well, it's not public knowledge yet," I leaned in closer. "Andra is currently in Kenya filming the Gastrafrique TV show. It's similar to what we do on Instagram already, but more like a scripted reality tv food critic show, slash cooking show, slash lifestyle. You get the picture."

"Word!? That's dope, Kobe!" She touched my arm. "Why aren't you there?"

"Well," I paused, hoping I wasn't giving up too much info too soon, "We're also opening the Gastrafrique restaurant here in Parque Place."

Her excitement was palpable and I must admit that shit made me proud as fuck.

Realizing how rude I'd been, I motioned towards Deidre who'd been standing idly checking her phone. "Let me introduce you two. Deidre this is Carmel. An," I paused to think of how I should introduce her, "an old friend from school. Carmel, this is Deidre Stark, the interior designer helping us come up with the dope design for the restaurant!"

"Damn, Kobe. You doing the damn thing," Carmel praised as she reached past me to shake Deidre's hand.

"Yeah, Andra and I are super excited about everything that's happening." I felt a tug of angst at the thought of Andra, feeling like my words were empty since I really didn't know how she felt about any of this, since she hadn't gotten around to sharing her feelings with me. Shrugging off my morose thoughts, I plastered on a thin smile at Carmel before adding, "It's all happening so fast. I've jumped into the deep end and am praying that all of the balls being juggled float."

Carmel's phone alerted. She glanced at it then at her watch before looking at me and Deidre. "I better get going. I actually have a product shoot scheduled that I need to get to."

"It was good seeing you, Carmel," I said, reaching in for another hug. "We need to get back over to the restaurant as well."

She stepped back from the embrace and I turned to leave.

She grabbed my hand, tugging back. "Do you mind if we exchange numbers? I'd really love to catch up with you. If that's cool."

I wrestled my lips down from what must have been the biggest Colgate smile ever. Be cool Kobe. "Absolutely!" I said, fumbling with my phone to quickly key in the digits she was calling out before hitting the call button, offering her a chance to lock my number in as well.

Carmel's hand still grasped mine, her hazel eyes twinkling with an infectious joy as our gazes locked, magnetizing us together.

I broke the connection first, tentatively wondering if I should ask her out. Hell why not? The Shay situation was a done deal. And Andra. Yeah... What about her? She didn't particularly care for Carmel back in high school. But so what? I wasn't feeling particularly cared for by her either. I squared my shoulders and just asked before Carmel walked away, "Maybe we could get dinner sometime this week or something?"

"I'd love to. Call me," Carmel said over her shoulder as she walked away.

Chapter 14 – Andra

♥

I'D FOLLOWED KAYLA'S DIRECTIONS for packing to a tee. Jeans. Loose-fitting, long-sleeved tops. Rubber soled shoes. Minimal accessories. It gave me an excuse to not get on the Peloton and ride with Kobe for our scheduled workout last night. I sent him a text message telling him that exact bullshit. I had to pack for the segment shoot out in the field.

The words in that message rang so hollow. His simple, "Ok," response felt like a dagger through my chest. I felt horrible for blowing our workout off, his calls, his messages, him... I hated blowing my best friend off. I missed Kobe —his laughter, his quirks, his steadiness. But after seeing the water droplets from his shower cascading down his tall, muscular form, I saw Kobe as I'd never allowed myself to see him—unveiled, raw, and breathtakingly fine. And his dick. My gawd. The things I couldn't stop thinking about doing to that... that.

I swallowed hard just thinking about it. This was Kobe—my best friend, my confidante. I was ashamed of how my feelings for him had shifted—like a camera lens refocusing. He no longer was just my best friend, but a man—compelling, captivating, desirable. My mind in regards to him was a whirlwind of questions and realizations. So I did what I always did when I found myself in uncharted territory. I either fucked away my feelings or avoided them. Kobe got the latter.

I threw myself into the harrowing task of packing. Just like Kayla had warned. And I was glad I did. Our small group and equipment was packed into three 4x4 Toyota Landcruiser Jeeps, which were comfortable enough during the first three-and-a-half hours of the road trip from Nairobi to the famed Maasai Mara big game reserve. The last hour, not so much.

"Hold on!" Our driver yelled over the intercom, just before we hit what felt like a crater as soon as the paved road gave way to a narrow one lane strip of red dirt.

The brightness of the red earth reminded me of Georgia red clay. *Home.* This felt like home. I instinctively played with the beaded bracelet, ever present on my arm.

We hit another bump and the driver's voice was barely audible over the loud roar of the diesel engine. He gave notice for us to brace ourselves as he warned, "The road is notoriously bad this time of year. Hold on!"

We all understood the purpose of the steel grab bars beside each seat as the jeep pitched sharply to the right as the driver navigated over the rougher terrain.

"Shit," Kayla yelled, juggling the phone wrenched from her fingers.

The camera man's "Oof," bellowed from deep in his chest when his body collided with the steel door of the cab.

"Fuck," flew from my lips as the side of my head connected with the grab bar before I could put up a hand to shield the impact.

We were all laughing at the ridiculousness of it all by the time the dirt road smoothed and we came to a stop in front of the Osero Lodge safari camp.

The word gorgeous couldn't describe the structure that appeared to be carved out of the lush foliage of the landscape. The Ngama Hills served as a backdrop for the beautiful, thatched roof of the lodge's welcome center.

The lush grounds of the property were sprawling and a swimming pool surrounded by deep pink and lavender flowers twinkled nearby. There were several stone pathways that diverged from the front of the resort style lodge, covered by awnings of thick vines with the same pink and violet petals interwoven.

In the distance, I could see what appeared to be tents. Each massive in size. They were a deep green canvas. Were it not for the attached porches decorated with heavy wooden patio furniture covered in richest jewel-colored fabrics, the structures would blend into the surrounding bush.

The rhythmic beat of tribal drums welcomed us. The music surrounded me, creating a sensory experience unlike anything I had ever encountered before. I was instantly connected to this place.

Moments later, we were greeted by several tall young men and a woman who introduced herself as Joanna, our concierge. She handed each of us a key. The studio made the arrangements with the lodge, pulling a few strings to accommodate our full crew and film equipment, so we were expected. The check in process was a breeze.

My attention was drawn to the tall men dressed in long wool cloaks of the most brilliant, checkered patterns of reds, blues, and fuchsias. Our concierge explained the patterned fabric were *shukas*, colorful robes worn by the Maasai people to ward off big game.

The only other clothing visible were the roughhewn leather sandals on their feet. But each of them wore the most intricately designed beadwork around their necks that I'd ever seen. No. Not true. I'd seen this sort of beadwork before.

I looked at my wrist, fingering the beaded bracelet, then back to the neck of the nearest man. My beaded bracelet, made from the beading on the doll my father had given me the last time I saw him. They were the same.

I'd made the bracelet years ago after I'd outgrown the doll. The toy had been long gone, but the beads were too pretty to throw away.

I was frozen, hearing nothing but his words... *"Here you go, ma'Baby! One that looks just like you! Brown butter toast! Now go play with your Massai warrior princess in your room while I talk to your mommy!"*

The whole scene took me back to the last time I'd seen him. *My father.* The last gift I'd received from him. That doll. The only clue to who he was. To his people?

The idea of searching for my dad had played at the edges of my mind since I'd arrived in Kenya. Each time, I'd shut the thoughts down. He didn't deserve any real estate in my mind. I'd blocked him out like he'd blocked me out all my life. But now...

This place gave me a sense of feeling tethered. Belonging. My skin was alive with the rush of a love that I knew years ago, but thought had died. Somehow this place made me yearn to feel my daddy's love again. The sensation overcame me. I stood on the precipice of tears, with a longing for my daddy I hadn't felt in years.

"Earth to Andra. Andra –"

I blinked away the moisture beginning to pool in my eyes, before turning to meet Kayla's smiling but concerned gaze.

"You good, girl?"

"Yeah. Yes." I stammered, "I'm just overwhelmed by the beauty of this place. I wasn't expecting," I waved my hand at the lodge, "*this.*"

"It is a lot to take in." She stood next to me, looking around at the site with deep appreciation on her face. "And the sunsets here are to die for. You know," she added thoughtfully, "It was pretty important to somebody high up the food chain at the studio that we shoot here because they spared no expense to add this last-minute segment to the show. This is costing a pretty penny."

"Who added the segment?" I asked her flat-out.

"I'm not sure. All the producer told me was that one of the higher-ups with big pockets wanted us to add the segment into the lineup."

She also shared that everything had been shifted around so that this segment would be aired during the season finale and we needed to get enough content for a full spread on the Gastrafrique Instagram page as a special online bonus before she excitedly added, "I don't care how it came to be. Shooting on location on the Maasai Mara is every director's dream! I can't wait to begin tomorrow."

"Me too," I agreed for reasons quite different from Kayla's.

At that very moment, I'd decided that I was going to find him, my father. Fortified with my decision, I was going to make the most of this trip. Find out as much as I could about the Maasai people. Maybe even find myself in the process. No script needed. I was going to put my all into this. A soul mission. I was going to leave it all on the Mara.

"Umm, Kayla," I said, pulling her from her reverie. I could tell she was thinking through the shot list for tomorrow.

Her head swiveled; eyes met mine with raised questioning brow.

"I have some creative thoughts about the episode. After we get settled, can we discuss over dinner?"

She looked at me appraisingly, nodding her head up and down slowly before responding in a half-smile as if she was seeing me for the first time. "Hell yeah. I've been waiting for the boss bitch Andra_B to show up!"

"What do you know about Andra_B?" I genuinely laughed at her reference to my IG handle.

"Girl, we get Instagram in the bush," she laughed, "Isn't that what all you Americans believe? We all live in the bush? Titties hanging. Baby strapped to the back. Basket on our head?"

Wide-eyed, I swatted her shoulder, "Stop that! We do not believe any of that! I am half Kenyan, ya' know!"

"No. I didn't know that." Now she was the one surprised. "Okay, my *Sistah*," she said. "Let's go get settled into these plush ass sultan's tents and meet back up, say in an hour?"

"That will be perfect," I paused to scan the pamphlet handed to each of us by the concierge, "looks like dinner in the open-air dining room will be served by then."

"Ok. An hour it is. Might even catch that sunset."

As the director, Kayla had full autonomy over the shot list. I was ecstatic to give my input.

She sat back from her plate, satisfied from the lamb chops that we'd both had double helpings of and took a sip of her rum and coke. "Ok, tell me what you're thinking for the episode."

I cleared my throat and sat back in my seat, placing the napkin across my plate. The words tumbled out without thought. I had the clearest vision of what I wanted to know about the Maasai Mara and my people. I was going to learn everything, up close and personal and the viewing public would learn it all through my eyes.

"As you know, the Maasai Mara is one of the most iconic wildlife reserves in East Africa, so I think we should start the segment on safari. It will be like a treasure hunt to find the Big Five. I want it to be filmed mocumentary style, a humorous parody if you will, as if the big game are hunting us to to make the episode funny at first, but to also soften the landing. I would then like to transition to total immersion into life with the Maasai people."

Kayla was again nodding slowly as the vision poured from my mouth, stopping me only to agree, "Yes. I like the light hand you're going for. We'll start off having a bit of fun in the bush, to set the stage for the heavy hitting content about who these people are and their important role in the history of the Rift Valley. Then we close it out on a high note. The food. That way we don't risk losing the viewers and we stay true to the essence of Gastrafrique. It's gotta be about the food."

"Right," I nodded, more seriously. "While on safari, I will be interviewing our driver, so he can share the majesty of the Mara. I also imagine, you and the team can get amazing b-roll footage for the show and great photos of the landscape and wildlife for the social media content to be used on Gastrafrique's IG."

At this point, Kayla was scribbling in the notepad she'd brought as I kept talking. "I want the footage with the Maasai people to really showcase their beauty and unique way of living. I want to focus on every aspect of their daily life, but I agree. Mainly on their food."

When I finally stopped talking, she put her pen down. "This is going to be an amazing segment," she said, splaying her hands wide, "I Can't wait to make your vision come alive. You should try your hand at directing. You're a natural."

I smiled. My exhilaration could not be explained in words. I wanted to share this feeling with someone, the gravity of my connection to this place. I wanted to tell Kobe. My heart immediately accelerated at the mere thought of him. As soon as we get back to Nairobi, I'm going to put my lust away and call him to apologize. I would just have to keep my feelings to myself. I valued our friendship too much to ruin it with my misplaced lust. In the meantime, I was bursting to share my suspected connection to the Maasai people.

Kayla had just taken another sip of her drink when I just said it. "My father is... was... Maasai."

She raised an eyebrow. "Was? I'm sorry to hear that."

"Oh no. I didn't mean he was dead. Well, I wouldn't know. I haven't seen him since I was four."

"I see," she said quietly, allowing me to continue.

"The last thing he gave me was a doll. Dressed in the clothes of the Maasai people," I said, holding up my wrist so she could see the bracelet and explaining where it came from. "I think he may be Maasai."

She moved her hand to cover mine, Her lip raising in a lopsided smile. "Then this is home coming. We must capture that."

We shot for two days straight on the Maasai Mara. Just as Kayla and I planned, the first day went off without a hitch. The lighthearted nature of the segment had us all laughing and jovial.

The driver knew everything about the animals and where they could typically be found. It made it easy to turn the whole segment into us being hunted by the big animals. With Kayla's direction and tricks of the camera, the action and our mock terror came off as planned.

The second day was a spiritual journey. My soul would be laid bare for everyone to see. In essence, I was tracing my roots through a profound experience of meeting the Maasai people and their, my, true culture. I, along with everyone watching the episode, would see myself fully in the context of being my father's child. I wasn't just another fatherless girl from Atlanta. My history was rich and full. The camera would bridge my two worlds.

My people were a patriarchal society, centered around their cattle, the primary source of food and wealth. Because the Maasai people were historically nomadic, they wore bright red or fuchsia robes that they were known for as protection, scaring many of the big animals away. Both the men and women adorned themselves with the same unique, colorful beaded jewelry that had been etched in my memory since childhood.

The more I learned over the course of recording the segments on the Maasai Mara, the more questions I had for him. I began hoping for the opportunity to ask him. Questions like, if it was the custom of Maasai men to take in all of his wife's offspring, even outside children, and treat them as his own, why did he abandon me? If the Maasai were known to be calm and courageous, then why would he leave me like a coward.

For me, the content and footage was heavy, but I did find some comic relief sitting with the local women in the Maasai encampment. We'd come to the part where the food of the Maasai would take center stage.

They welcomed me into the enkang settlement and an elder showed me how to make fire. A few of the women cooked beef over the open flame and fried yams in roughhewn steel pans. The stew was not unlike most beef stews I'd seen and tasted before but I was surprised that cow's milk instead of a starch was used to thicken it. We highlighted the similarities of the traditional Maasai stew to a Russian beef stroganoff.

That was where the similarities ended. When the elder cook pulled out a bowl of bright red liquid, all of the other ladies of the tribe appeared to bow their heads in silent reverence to her and the stew.

Kayla gasped and I faintly heard her inward groan. When I looked over, her face was piqued as if she would wretch. Her eyes were transfixed on the bowl; its contents now being poured into the stew, turning it a milky pink in color. Even though many of the tribe spoke English, the elders did not. I turned to one of the younger ladies to ask what was poured into the bowl.

"It is cows' blood," she said, covering her lips to hide her giggle at the stricken look on my face. "It is used in many ceremonial rituals. Today, it is to honor you," she looked at Kayla briefly. Kayla gave her a nod as if giving permission for the girl to finish. "Kayla informed that you are possibly connected by birth to the Maa people. We want to welcome you into our tribe, Sister." She bowed to me over praying hands and my heart was laid bare.

Right there amid the women of the Maasai tribe. I ate the beef and drank the blood, fully embracing my heritage as a half Maasai, wholly proud woman.

No longer did I feel like an imposter in my Kenyan heritage. In knowing these people, I gained a sense of knowledge of self, an answer to the open question mark of my life. Who am I? I am Maasai. And right then and there, I dropped the cloak of the messy unknown part of me on the Mara. It was time to close the circle and find my father.

Chapter 15 –Kobe

I COULDN'T BELIEVE IT, here I was out on a date with Carmel after all these years. We'd spent our 11th grade year in a relationship. If you could call it that. We'd really spent almost a year arguing over my friendship with Andra, until she broke up with me after prom. Rightfully so I guess, after I'd left her at the prom to tend to Andra, who'd caught her date Luke fucking a broad in the stairwell.

We'd tried again a couple of times after that but lost touch when I took a leap year to study abroad at Le Cordon Bleu in France. I'd only seen her once since then and it was at Andra's graduation from Spelman. They were classmates in college but hung in vastly different circles.

I studied Carmel's shapely ass as she walked in front of me across the swanky lounge on the way to our seats. She moved as gracefully now as she did walking in the Miss Teen pageants she was so into back in the day. Every dude in the spot had their eyes glued to her long legs enhanced by the short flowy dress and wedge sandals she wore.

R&B was playing throughout the speakers in the lounge. As she waited for me to pull out her chair, Carmel swayed her hips to the beat. Her eyes slowly raked up my body, locking on mine, holding the gaze briefly before taking her seat.

Damn. She was fine. The years had been good to her. Narrow hips had transformed. Not thick for Atlanta standards, but enough to hold on to. Small waist, defined arms, and lips as pouty as her pert cleavage tastefully on display in the low cut of the wrap dress she wore.

I took my seat across from her as the waitress leaned in to take our drink orders. We both had to damn near shout for her to hear us over the music. Communication across the table was impossible. Carmel leaned across to yell something at me. After I leaned closer and she attempted three times to tell me something to no avail, she stood squeezing through the tight space between our table and the next and sat in my lap on the bench seating.

"I was asking if you'd ever been here before?" she said, leaning into me, close enough that I could feel her breath tickle the fine hairs in my ear. Her floral fragrance pleasantly tickled my nose.

"I haven't. But Andra reviewed this place on Gastrafrique last year. I've been wanting to check it out."

Carmel's body tensed slightly, eyes narrowed and shifted quickly at the mention of Andra's name. She quickly recovered and turned her torso into me, to whisper, "Let's get out of here."

"You sure? We just ordered drinks."

"I'm sure. As a matter of fact, I noticed Brewster's right around the corner. It's nice out tonight. We can go grab an ice cream cone. Walk and Talk."

"Cool. I can dig an ice cream cone, right now!"

We did just that. It felt like high school all over again. We'd gotten our cones to go and decided to walk to Skyview, the big Ferris wheel by Centennial Park to people watch and catch up.

She told me about the cushy job she'd had as operations manager for one of those big-name beauty companies, when she decided to risk it all, and step out on faith to start her own brand.

"So that's how you started Porified?" I asked.

"Yep. Once I realized that I was putting all my energy into a company and its products that I couldn't even use on my own hair," she pointed up at her natural coils as exhibit A, "I started making my own products in my kitchen. Next thing you know, I was making products for my friends. And then things just started taking off from there."

"That's dope as fuck!" I said genuinely in awe of her story. "It's similar to how Gastrafrique blew up. Though I must say, most of the credit goes to Andra and her social media skills."

"Well I've followed Gastrafrique for a while now," she slowed and stepped in front of me placing a tentative hand on my chest. She tilted her head slightly to the side looking up at me, the index finger of her free hand gingerly tapping her lips before sweetly saying, "Chef_Ko_Bae is the star of the show, though."

She was so close and smelled so good. I had to pull myself out of her delicious amber haze. I was flattered but couldn't take the credit like that.

"Naw, Andra gets the props. As a matter of fact, I've been struggling trying to keep up with creating content and every-thing while she's been away shooting," I offered a chagrined smile. "I feel like I'm letting our followers down because I'm not engaging with them like I should. I knew she did a lot, but man," I said, rubbing the back of my head, "Andra is a genius at that shit."

This time, Carmel didn't even try to mask her eye roll. She turned back forward and began walking again, moving slightly ahead of me. I should have taken note of that little display as a red flag but that ass took over.

When she finally spoke, it was over her shoulder. "You know, I'm pretty savvy on IG, right?" She stopped walking, pulled out her phone and tapped a few times on the screen. She held her phone up eye-level so I could see the highly curated, white, and neutral palette of the Porified profile gallery.

"It fits," I said, taking advantage of the stillness and pulling her into a loose hug. "As a matter of fact, if profiles had a smell, yours would be a heady mixture of sage, bergamot, and vanilla. Warm and satisfying."

"I like that," she said, tapping her fingers to her lips again in thought. "You should let me help you with Gastrafrique."

"I don't know. I'm sure it'll be fine once Andr—"

"I'm sure Andra's busy." She clipped, raising an eyebrow. "You said she's filming in Kenya, right?"

"Y—, yeah," I fumbled over my words. A quick surprised laugh escaped my lips in reaction to her sudden switch up.

"Well it's settled. I can help you with Gastrafrique. You know what they say. The algorithm wants its content!" She giggled, switching back to playfulness in the blink of an eye. Still a bit disconcerted but choosing to brush it off, I agreed to let her teach me a few things.

We continued our stroll around Centennial Park. By the time we'd made it to the Ferris wheel, she'd already given me several pointers on how to overcome my self-consciousness in front of the camera. We had already planned another date to meet up and work on some content for both our brands together by the time we were several stories up on the Ferris Wheel.

A week had gone by before Carmel and I had our second date. I'd invited her to my condo and cooked two red snappers for our dinner. Admittedly, I was flexing my culinary muscle and fried the fish to golden perfection, topped with confetti red, green, yellow, and orange peppers, steeped in an herb infused olive oil and vinaigrette dressing. I was putting the mashed yucca on the side and finishing the plating when she knocked.

"It's open!" I yelled and as she walked in, Crazy-Balls bounded from the bedroom. She'd been so quiet, chilling on her bed with a chew toy, that I'd forgotten to close the room door. I chased behind her to yoke Balls up by her collar, knowing she'd probably try to corner Carmel like she'd done with Shay and every other woman other than Andra who'd come over.

To my surprise, Carmel walked right up to Balls, shifted the wine bottle that she carried in her right hand to her left and bent down to introduce herself to my dog with a "Hey pretty girl," and a scratch under her chin. I really had my mouth wide open because Balls actually let her then loafed back into the room and laid back down.

"Well shit." I said, surprised.

"What?" Carmel asked, gazing quizzically at the dumb look on my face.

"Umm... nothing. Just didn't take you for a dog person." I sure as hell wasn't going to say that Balls didn't like any woman other than Andra. Carmel might be a keeper. I liked her and all before. That increased tenfold knowing my dog was cool with her too.

"Yeah. I absolutely love dogs. Been thinking about getting Jewels one, but that girl isn't responsible enough for a pet yet." Jewels was her six-year-old daughter. She'd shown me pictures of the pretty little girl with pigtails on our first date.

She walked past me into the kitchen to sit the wine bottle she'd brought on the counter. Her eyes bugged when she spotted the plates. "Oh *dammmnn*. I see why you couldn't open the door for me." She whipped out her phone and started snapping pics of the plates. "See this is Gastrafrique right here! You mind if I post these?"

"Naw. Go ahead. Just send them to me so I can post them on Gastrafrique too," I said, proud of my handiwork.

"How about I just tag @Gastrafrique in my post?"

"Cool," I shrugged, giving no other thought to her question.

We ate dinner and polished off the bottle of wine she'd brought. As we were clearing the table, she piped up in her bubbly bright sort of way to explain an idea she had for a brand collaboration with Gastrafrique and Porified on Instagram.

"The headline could be something like, 'When your skin care is so good and natural, the *Gastra*-Freaks at Gastrafrique rave about it!'"

It was cute. *Silly...* But I got the vision. I must have been loose off the two glasses of wine I'd drank because I blindly agreed to the idea. When she'd further explained the vision that we'd need to look the part of a couple doing their nightly routine before bed in front of the bathroom mirror where I'd be shirtless and in my boxers. And she'd be stripped down to bra and panties with one of my oversized white button downs. I wholeheartedly agreed to the idea.

By the time we'd polished off the rest of the contents of the wine, ring lights and cameras were set up in the bathroom and her long, toned legs were peeking out of my shirt that just skimmed her ass.

The sight of her half naked in my bathroom made it hard to focus on the task of recording the content, but I followed her lead and before long we were clowning and acting out the slogan. At some point she'd whipped out several posh containers of creams and face scrubs. All laid out on my bathroom counter and we got in full character as we shot a reel. She'd even licked the thick creamy concoction meant to gently clean your face off my cheek.

Even in the wine induced haze, I subconsciously knew I should've ran the idea past Andra before going ahead with it – but by the time Carmel worked her magic editing, adding transitions and music, the video was fucking dope. Plus, Andra was yet to return any of my calls anyway, so I had zero fucks to give.

We finally wrapped just after midnight. Carmel scheduled the campaign in Hootsuite to launch tomorrow at 11am across both the Gastrafrique and Porified social media platforms.

Balls and I walked Carmel to the door. I reached in for a friendly hug but was surprised when she leaned in and kissed me. Keeping my cool, I reciprocated and pulled her close. Her body felt good as it molded into mine. Thoughts of her toned legs in my bathroom made her body feel real good. Too good. I had to mentally coach the monster growing in my pants back down.

I didn't want to let her go but standing in the open door with my dick on brick while Carmel was trying to go home wasn't a good look. As if reading my thoughts, she smiled and backed away, giving me one last look before reaching down to scratch behind Ball's ear saying goodbye. I wasn't surprised to find Balls watching me with an understanding expression as I watched Carmel head down the hall.

As I pulled into my parking spot at 1679 Parque Place, My phone rang. It was Andra. Finally, I thought, hurrying to put the Range Rover in park to answer her call. It had been two weeks of missing each other via phone and I should have been pissed, but I was excited that she'd most likely seen the post by now. The engagement numbers were already off the charts. The video was already going viral and had only been up for a few hours.

I wanted to see the excitement on Andra's face and almost declined the voice call to Facetime her but opted against. It was a good thing that I did. Before I could even say hello, she was launching into me.

"What the fuck is this bullshit ass post, Kobe!"

"Yo, Anj—" I said, taken totally aback at the anger in her voice.

"Don't fucking *'Anj'* me. You and this... this throwback," she seethed, so mad she could barely get the words out. , "Y'all all over Gastrafrique eating face pudding off of each other and shit. That's what the fuck we doing now?"

"Face pudding? Andra, what - ?"

"You all over our shit, A FOOD BLOG, while this corny bitch is licking face cream off ya' cheek! We're not sponsored by her skincare company. Make it make sense, Kobe!"

Ohhh... I chuckled at Andra's reference to Carmel's all-natural face cream. "Let me explain –."

"I'm waiting."

"So, I've been struggling to keep up with the social media content. You know I'm not good at that shit. That's your departme -"

"So you just go and rebrand without talking with me?"

"Umm... No. It's a collaboration. Brands do it all the time, Andra," I paused, getting annoyed with her cutting me off, "As I was saying, I couldn't get you on the phone. Guess you've been too... busy or something," I paused again, knowing the 'or something' I really wanted to call her out on probably had something to do with some random dude she'd met on set. I quickly recovered, stating, "That's neither here nor there. When I couldn't get you on the phone, Carmel offered to help. Her Porified face products are 100% natural. Edible even." I said, voice raising to match hers. "We promote food. She promotes food like products. Get it –"

"That is the stupidest shit I've heard in my fucking life, Kobe. She doesn't even have 100,000 followers. Who is this little collabo really benefiting. Not us. Seems a little bit opportunistic to me!"

Opportunistic? Andra was taking this shit too far. I was too stunned to cut her off.

"Then she all up on you licking you and shit and both of you half naked in your bathroom. That. Is. Not. Our Brand." Andra reined in her composure but clapped between each word for emphasis. She stopped abruptly, taking in a deep gulp of air, and blowing it out shakily. She sounded as though she was choking back tears when she softly said, "And y'all were looking mighty damn... chummy in that mirror. Where did you even drag her ass up from, again?"

The pained emotion in Andra's words cut through my irritation, bringing my anger down and concern for her up. For reasons I couldn't quite understand, I felt guilty talking about Carmel. Choosing my words carefully, I continued, "I ran into her a few weeks back at Parque Place. Around the corner from the restaurant..." My voice trailed off, the excitement about the restaurant space, staling at the realization that Andra and I had been so disconnected, that I hadn't even been able to share with her how amazing it was or anything. The uncomfortable silence between us lingered.

When she finally spoke again, her voice came out in a whisper. It was solemn. Almost as if to herself. "Y'all make a really cute couple."

I didn't know what to say. I wasn't sure if Andra's anger, sadness... I couldn't tell which was about our brand or about Carmel. I was still processing the whole conversation when Andra finally said, "Um, I gotta go."

The phone line went dead.

Chapter 16 – Andra

W E'D JUST GOTTEN BACK from filming on the Maasai
Mara in the early morning hours. Filming in the studio
resumed immediately and it was frenzied because we had to get
the schedule back on track to make up for the time spent on the
unplanned segment.

I'd made the decision to do some digging to find my father. I
knew it would be hard because all I had was a name. My mother
never shared intimate details about him or his family with me.

Between takes and after filming for the day, I'd poured through
people finder websites. Making a few calls to vital records, I had
compiled a list of numbers that could be his. I'd called them all
except one with no luck.

Energy zinged through me as I fingered the paper with the last
number scrawled on it. It seemed different. So much so that I
decided to take a quick scroll through IG first to calm my nerves
and temper my disappointment if this last number was a dead end.

The image of myself as that little girl who sat by the window all those years ago waiting for her daddy to come back home made me a little sad. But that feeling didn't last long.

I was about to call Kobe to apologize for being distant and avoiding him, to gather my nerves to call that last number. I was going to have to grow some balls and explain my feelings to him. I didn't quite understand them, but I knew that I wanted to try to explain. Plus, we needed to be on speaking terms in the event that this last number did belong to my father so I needed to catch him up on everything that I had discovered about my connection to my father.

I was getting ready to call him when I saw it. A co-branded post between Gastrafrique and Porified. What the hell? Oh. We needed to talk alright. Kobe had some explaining to do! He answered on the third ring and I proceeded to light his ass on fire.

I was in my feelings. Kobe –. No, *Carmel* had me fucked up. This bitch just shows up out of the blue and thinks she's about to jump on the Gastrafrique bandwagon? Not no, but HELL no! Hell. Fucking. No. And Kobe… his ol' pushover ass doesn't even see how this tramp is using him. Just like she tried to use him for clout back in high school.

She was always trying to get him to buy her shit. Lying about him getting her nails done. Lying about him buying her class ring…

All lies. And I knew this because Mrs. Abara had put a whole halt to that shit before it went down.

Still, her opportunistic ass wore his letterman jacket every day to save face. She wore that shit even after he had stopped fucking with her after prom. *Who the fuck does that?*

After hanging up on Kobe, I needed to do something with the pent-up frustration that I felt over what was happening to us. Our friendship and business. Over how close he and Carmel looked. Together...

I channeled the anxiety and angst into the other situation that caused a different kind of angst. Calling the last number that could possibly connect me to my father.

Letting out a long-resigned sigh, I slumped down at a corner table in the back of the break room and dialed the number. As soon as I pressed my cell phone to my ear, a tall figure walked into the breakroom—it was the strange man who'd made an appearance on set weeks ago. He hadn't noticed me in the back as he was headed directly towards the coffee machine near the entrance. Waiting for the call to begin ringing, I had a brief second to take him in. He was all business, dark suit pristine. Gray hair and beard framing the distinguished features of a man in charge.

The shrill, metallic sound of the call ringing vibrated my eardrum, startling me because I had been mindlessly watching him. *It rang again.* As if on cue, he paused. Still not noticing me, he fisted his phone that rang simultaneously from his pocket. His face wrinkled as he looked at the screen before tapping to answer it.

"Hello," he answered.

I gasped.

At the sound, he turned, noticing me for the first time. Our eyes locked. Mine on eyes that even across the expanse of space, mirrored my own. The air was sucked from the room.

I watched his lips move in sync with the auditory sound of the hello from the voice through the speaker on my phone. It resounded clear and in stereo through my speaker.

The break room became extremely small as I sat suspended in the threshold of two worlds at once. A simple *'hello'* and I was transported to our kitchen thirty plus years ago. My four- year-old self standing in a chair, pressing the receiver of the big yellow wall phone to my ear as my mom smiled on from across the room. *"Hello, ma' baby,"* he said back then.

He cleared his throat. Again, I heard it in clear Dolby digital.

Time stopped. The hello was suspended between us.

The deep baritone of his voice tickled my eardrum much like the ringing did. My eyes were glued to him, but my mind played the sound and the feeling of his voice over and over again.

Maybe I was losing my mind. To hear three hellos simultaneous-ly. One from the past. Two right now, live and in person and over my phone. All simultaneously as if the time and space continuum had folded in on itself and I, we, were stuck in the middle.

The man in the suit, the distinguished gray beard had the power to make an entire studio pop to attention at his sheer presence. The mystery man had the power to magically manifest himself into this breakroom and be on the receiving end of a call to the last piece of hope I had of finding him. This man standing right in front of me, right now and in real life, was the same man who'd abandoned me years ago.

The world around me started moving at a different speed. Gravity was restored. The air whooshed back into my lungs as understanding flooded my senses. My emotions swirled. Too fast. I was a caged animal seeking escape. My gaze darted towards the exit. I had to get out of here.

Clutching my phone in one hand, I used the other to push away from the table, stumbling in haste. I ran from the room. Past the studio. Past familiar faces of the cast who looked at me in concern. I kept going.

Hot tears began to singe my eyes. My lungs burned as I tried to breath past the lump in my throat. I pushed through the back door of the studio sucking the cool late afternoon air into my chest as I pressed my back against the wall of the building for balance.

Kobe's face flashed across my mind as I balled over the knot in my stomach. His was the only face and place that made sense to me right now. I needed my best friend. The argument with him earlier, played on repeat. I fumbled with the phone, dialing his number. *Would he take my call? Was he still mine... my friend?* Everything was so confusing right now.

The phone rang three times. *Kobe please pick up.* I thought, panic starting to well up in me again. His voicemail. *Shit.* Tears now fully streaming down my face. I needed to keep moving. I ran around the building, intending to call an uber back to my condo. I was so blinded by my tears; I didn't see the black SUV until Okiyo called my name. *How was he here?* I hadn't called for a ride. Had no intentions of calling him for a ride.

I was surprised to see him step out of the driver's seat instead of Deke. He grabbed my elbow and used his wide chest to shield me from any onlookers as he guided me to the front passenger door. Hopping in beside me in the driver seat. He offered no words, yet his silence calmed me as we drove away from the studio.

I couldn't help but wonder what he already knew about my father—who may have told him of our connection in order for him to be so well informed? What else did he know about this stranger who had only just revealed himself after 30 years of absence? The questions bubbled up in my mind like a swarm of bees as twilight descended around us.

The car ride felt like it lasted an eternity as I kept struggling with my thoughts, the questions, my feelings—the confusion, the anger, the hurt all mixed together in one big boiling pot of emotion ready to explode.

I pulled out my phone, hands trembling, and tried to call Kobe again. Still no answer. On top of everything else that was swirling through my mind, the thought occurred that he may have been with Carmel. The thought turned my mood bleaker. Abandoned now by the only man in my life who hadn't. I felt empty.

My tears had dried on the unfamiliar ride away from the studio. It was quite some time that we'd ridden in silence before I realized we weren't heading towards my condo. Somehow, Okiyo seemed to understand without needing any words that I really didn't want to be alone.

Eventually we pulled up to some nondescript building in an obscure alleyway. He turned, staring at my rigid profile for a few seconds across the passenger seat. "Would you like a bit of privacy, to try and call him again?"

I knew he'd meant Kobe, based on our conversation after leaving Giraffe Manor weeks ago. I looked away; eyes focused on the door of the building. "No...," I spoke quietly. Throwing up a wall to shut off all thoughts of a father who'd been absent for 30 years and a best friend that I had feelings for who quite possibly had feelings for another.

I turned to look at Okiyo. He gave me a lopsided smile then completely surprised me by unexpectedly reaching over to release my seatbelt. I looked up at him in disbelief; the secret service nigga actually smiled.

He got out and walked around to open my door.

"Come on," he said, placing the usual hand in the small of my back, ever the protector, leading us to the singular metal door on the outside of the building. He gave what sounded like a secret knock. When the door was opened, he ushered me inside an opulent room seeming straight out of a James Bond movie.

"A speakeasy," I said looking up at him through slanted eyes before smiling knowingly. "I would expect nothing less from you."

"I figured you could use a drink."

"You figured right," I said, taking my seat in the leather Chippendale chair he'd pulled out for me in the low seating area. And drink I did. "Two old fashions on the rocks," I spoke over the soft jazz playing in the background to the waiter who'd showed up as if on cue to take our orders.

"Old Fashions?" Okiyo said, eyes raised at the drinks, assuming I was ordering for him as well.

"Those two are for me. Order your own."

He laughed openly for the first time in my presence, as he relaxed back into his seat. "The lady knows what she wants." He tipped his head at me, then back to the waiter. "I'll have a glass of Opus One."

I found solace in the smooth music and the strong drink that flowed freely; it all felt like a much-needed escape from reality. Okiyo turned out to be great company. Before long, I was seriously buzzing from the alcohol. When I went to order another round, Okiyo signaled no to the waiter and instructed him to close out the tab.

"It's time I get you home, Andra. You have an early meeting with the boss in the morning."

"Boss," I slurred. "What boss?"

"Your father. I work for your father."

And there it was, the answer to how he seemed to know everything that went on earlier. I was stunned into silence but followed him back to the truck. Again, this was all too much, but too much alcohol simultaneously numbed my brain, and fueled the white-hot rage that was flowing through my body.

I leaned heavily against Okiyo as he led me through the lobby entrance of my condo. Ever the fucking gentleman.

Even in my tipsiness, I noticed the look exchanged between Okiyo and the same female concierge from the night I'd arrived. He offered her an almost imperceptible wink and her narrowed eyes softened as she offered a seductive smile meant only for him. He remained silent as she pushed a button to open the security turnstile so that we moved unimpeded to the elevator beyond.

His solid frame felt like an anchor as we rode up the elevator. He smelled of citrus and all man. The clear lust in ol' girl's eyes below needed no explanation. Okiyo was fucking fine. And he would do just fine for me to fuck away the stress from this fucked up day.

When we reached my front door he'd taken my key to open it. I wrapped my arms around him and tried to kiss him... He pulled back gently but firmly. *Oh. He's playing hard to get. Okay.* I thought.

Not used to being turned down, I continued pushing my body into his inviting him into my apartment with every move until he regained his footing and put some distance between us. He was firm, but never broke composure— "As tempting as the invitation is, Ms. Bainswright, there are lines in the sand, that not even the sea will cross. We should call it a night."

He stepped back, turned, and walked away. I watched his retreating back in disbelief.

Business as usual, he called over his shoulder, "Your meeting with your father is at 10am. I will be here promptly at 9:30 to retrieve you."

Chapter 17 –Kobe

♥

THE WHOLE BLOW UP with Andra over that damned IG post had left my mind in a proper spin. As if the day hadn't already started off on the wrong foot, I made my way through the back of the restaurant towards my sanctuary - the office. Instead of peace, what greeted me was pure pandemonium.

The back door had been kicked in. For a second I just stood there taking in the bent door frame, the busted lock, and the battered door. It looked as though either a dude with a size 18 steel-toed boot or a battering ram had gotten into an entanglement with the door.

I knew better than to touch anything so not to contaminate what surely was a crime scene, immediately reaching for my cell to dial 911. We hadn't even opened yet and motherfuckers were already breaking into the joint.

As I gave the requested information to the operator so that a unit could be dispatched, a wave of anxiety hit me as I remembered we'd just had all the kitchen equipment delivered. Fuck. The word exploded in my brain. It didn't take a major investigation to see that all that shit was gone.

The next call I made was to the security company. I needed to know why the freaking alarm didn't go off.

"Mr. Abara, we assure you that the alarm was not set."

"Yes it was," I argued. "I set it myself."

The motherfucker on the other end sighed as if he was frustrated with me.

"Get somebody out here ASAP to take a look at this piece of shit security system," I yelled before banging the end call button.

No sooner than I hung up, I heard my name being called from the front of the restaurant. *Fuck.* I forgot my mom was coming by to help me brainstorm the menu. I rushed up front to head her off before she saw the damage.

"Oh, *ma'Baby*," she said, eyes amazed at how the restaurant space was coming along. I headed her off before she could make it through the threshold leading to the offices. Undaunted, she opened her arms wide to greet me as she swept her eyes around the space. "Ohhh... Kobena! This is sooooo nice," she gushed, heavy Ghanaian accent unchecked in my familiar presence. "I *cah'not* wait to make some *majeek* with you on this menu..."

The excitement in her voice trailed when she noticed the look on my face and my eyes shifted past her to the officers who were walking in the door. My cell phone rang at the same time. *Andra.* Not now. I'm sure she had more words about the IG post that I'd since taken down, but I couldn't deal with that right now. Immediately after I'd sent her to voicemail, she called right back. I'd have to call her back.

"You Mr. Abara?" The first officer greeted. Walking in my direction and tipping his head at my mother.

"Yeah," I responded, placing my ringer on silence before dropping it in my pocket and reaching to shake the officer's hand.

"Mind telling me what happened?"

The other officer tipped his hat as well, "I'll have a look around while you tell officer Jackson what happened," he said, moving past his partner, my mother and I.

"Sure," I waved him to the back, "The damage is back there."

"What has happened?" My mother said, rushing to place her hand on my chest as if checking my vitals.

Partially to her. Partially to the officer standing in front of me, I ran down to them what I had walked into just over an hour ago.

"I let myself into the front door and was walking to the office when I noticed that the back door was kicked in."

"Did you notice anything missing?"

"Yeah. A lot of shit," I muttered, exasperated. Wiping a hand down my face to calm my building anger. "We just got a delivery of all the industrial kitchen equipment yesterday. All of that appears to be gone. Motherfu—" I paused, correcting myself as I remembered my mom was standing right there. Head volleying between me and the officer as if watching a game of tennis. "The mofo's even took the garbage disposal." I finished shaking my head.

Officer Jackson walked back into the open space of the bar area, notebook in hand. He looked at his partner with a knowing look as he turned on me and asked, "Mr. Abara, is there an alarm system in this place?"

"Yeah." I said, looking back and forth hesitantly at the two officers who now were viewing me suspiciously. "I called the monitoring service just before you two got here to ask why the alarm hadn't gone off."

"Interesting," Officer Jackson stated, deadpan look on his face.

"Funny thing is, the door does appear to have been kicked in, but the deadbolt wasn't engaged."

"Meaning?" I asked.

"Meaning, there really was no need to kick in a door if the deadbolt isn't engaged. Any petty criminal looking to score, could have just picked the lock, or jimmied it with a credit card."

"I locked that door myself and set the alarm myself, so I'm not sure what you are implying."

"No implying Mr. Abara. Just stating the facts."

At that point, my mother chimed in, "My son is no criminal and we resent the improper implication. I suggest you take the report and go make yourselves useful and file it!" The queen had spoken.

As soon as the officers left, the front door opened again and in walked Carmel. *Shit.* One, I was about to have to explain again, what had just happened. Two, I was praying that my mom didn't remember Carmel. She couldn't stand her when we dated back in high school.

No such luck. Before I could even greet Carmel properly and ask my mother if she remembered her, my mom was already being petty.

"*Oh no, Kobe.* Is that that girl?" my mother asked, an entreating look in my direction, in the most inconspicuous whisper. She knew full well anybody between here and the parking lot could hear the shade dripping off her voice.

"Mrs. Abara," Carmel oozed, walking towards my mother, arms wide for a hug. "It's been ages since I've seen you."

My mother's response, the most tepid hug I'd ever seen.

"Mmmhmmm…" she interjected, narrowing her eyes at me over Carmel's shoulder.

I ended up having to repeat what happened with the break in two more times before me and mom were able to actually even start on the menu. Once again to Carmel, who was almost in tears with concern and again to the insurance company who I'd had to file the claim for the stolen equipment. While I was in the office doing that, I could hear snippets of my mom and Carmel's conversation from upfront.

"Oh so you were here with Kobe last night?" My mom asked.

"No. He made me dinner at his apartment last night."

"Oh he did?" My mom asked again. Voice oozing sweetness as she stealthily grilled Carmel. "So you and my baby seeing each other now?"

"Well I wouldn't call it seeing each other. Not yet anyways. But we've been spending time together."

"Like time in the restaurant?"

"Um. Sure."

Carmel's answer trailed off as I walked back into the room.

"Alright. Business handled." I stated, rubbing my hands together, smiling ruefully back and forth between the two. "Hopefully you ladies were able to catch up a bit?" I said, brows raised apprehensively as I looked between the two of them. For a second, neither spoke then they started at the same time.

"Kobe, I'm gonna head—"

"*Mmm'yes.* Me and Andra... Oh pardon me. Carmel and I were just catching up. You'll have to forgive me dear. I'm not used to my son having any women around other than dear old Andra. You do remember Andra don't you?"

"Umm, yes." Carmel's brow pinched and her lips pressed into a thin line before her breath whizzed out in a miffed sigh. "Of course, I know Andra. How could anybody forget her?" Her brief look of dismay was quickly replaced with a grin that didn't quite reach her eyes as she turned to me. "Me and your mother were catching up and she told me you two are going to be working on the menu today so I'm going to go and let you two get to it." Carmel turned on her heels and was out the door before I could give her a hug goodbye. I stared after her for a moment, still thinking about the look on her face when she answered my mother's question.

Shrugging off the exchange that had just happened, I turned to my mother and asked, "You ready to get to it old lady?"

My mother swatted at my head, in response to me calling her old. I side-stepped her lick, laughing at her half-hearted attempt. After we'd finished laughing and prepared to go into my office to pour over ideas about the menu, she stopped short and looked back at the door that Carmel had just left out of. A look I couldn't quite read crossed her face. She shrugged it off before following me to the back.

A couple of hours later we were putting our finishing touches on the menu when she sat back and looked at me with a bit of concern on her face.

"That *gyul* has always been jealous of yours and Andra's friendship. I don't trust her. Never have, Kobe." She paused, looking at me for a reaction. At my raised eyebrows she continued. "She never liked Andra when you all were younger. You had your nose all open to that skinny heifer, but I could see it. The slick comments she'd say about Andra. The eyerolls she'd give when she thought no one was looking. I never liked that girl. Still don't. Something shady about her just can't put my finger on it." My mother paused, contemplating something, then shaking her thoughts away. "Nevermind her. Gastrafrique has a menu!" She smiled, reaching in to pat my cheek. "I'm so proud of you, my son."

Chapter 18 – Andra

♥

I MADE EVERY EFFORT to maintain my composure while Okiyo drove us to my father's estate, which was only a short distance away. I felt relieved that he didn't mention my actions from the previous night, and honestly, I didn't want to bring it up either. I had consumed alcohol excessively, and it had greatly affected my emotional state. My entire world felt shaken as a result.

I chose to give myself grace and was glad he didn't take my bait. It had been way too easy in the past for me to fuck my feelings away. Keeping things bottled up and superficial was my way. No entanglements, no hurt feelings, no broken hearts. No more. Today, I planned to confront my bullshit. Today was the day I'd confront the man who had taught me what rejection and abandonment felt like. I was going to get answers from the very source of my brokenness.

It was surreal. I was finally here meeting my father for the first time. I'd secretly dreamed about this day for years. Outwardly, I hated him for what he'd done to me. But in the loneliness of night, tucked away from the world, I imagined what it would feel like to hug him and hear his voice. I wasn't quite sure if today would be the dream, or quite possibly a nightmare, come true.

As we made our way up a lengthy driveway and came to a halt at a security gatehouse, my nerves overwhelmed me. We were ushered inside the gate of the vast compound by two security guards who checked our IDs before allowing us entry.

During the many rides back and forth from the studio and my condo, I had seen the rooftops of palatial family homes tucked away behind concrete walls and armed security guards. I'd imagined they were the homes of dignitaries or entertainers who'd come to Kenya to buy up the lush lands to put summer homes on. Never in a million years did I think the gates would be opened to me.

As we drove further into the property, my emotions surged. My mouth gaped. Disbelief. Shock. Anger. All intensified as I took in my surroundings. *This motherfucker was rich RICH.*

My head was spinning at the sheer number of questions running through it. *Who was this man?* Bigger question, *Why had he left my mother to take care of me by herself?* I didn't grow up poor in Atlanta, but compared to this, I guess I did.

Anger now consumed me. Evelyn Bainswright worked her ass off to give me a comfortable life. And he was over here living like royalty. *Wait. Was my father an African king? A chief, maybe?*

More questions. I took a deep breath to cool myself down, blowing it out so hard that Okiyo's eyes jerked up to the rearview mirror to see if I was about to implode.

When we finally came to a stop at the end of the driveway, the contemporary white concrete and glass house loomed in front of us. It was breathtaking. The stone steps were flanked with manicured topiaries that lead to a set of double ornate wooden doors reminiscent of castles in medieval Europe.

The doors swung open and two servants... I mean actual servants dressed in formal maid and butler outfits, complete with white aprons and penguin tails rushed down the stairs to greet us. The housekeeper ushered us inside. While the butler took care of the car.

Okiyo's booming voice startled me when he good naturedly chided our escort, "Oh stop with this formal nonsense. You're just putting on for company, Bishara."

"That's Mrs. Bishara to you!" She swatted his arm, giving him a sly smile. "Mind *ya'mannahs* chap." Based on the easy camaraderie between the housekeeper, Mrs. Bishara, and Okiyo, it was obvious he was a well-known fixture around the property.

"Ah, manners. Right. Let me start by introducing you to Ms. Bainswright." And in true Okiyo form, he bowed with a flourish, presenting me to the housekeeper.

She made a "Tsk" sound towards him. "Get out the way, you handsome devil. I know who she be." At that Mrs. Bishara gave me the most welcoming, grandmotherly smile. Placing a soft hand on my elbow before slightly bowing herself. "Ms. Andra, welcome child. We've been waiting for the day you come."

Too overcome by her kindness and too surprised by her words, I could only smile before looking at Okiyo with questioning eyes. He winked, offering a slight upturn to his lips before his face returned to the unreadable mask that was normally there. It comforted me just the same.

Mrs. Bishara led us through the grandiose foyer down a long hallway of rich white marble floors and lined with intricately carved doors—it was Kenyan opulence at its finest! Before long we came to a stop where the hallway intersected another that ran perpendicular to the one we were on. I swiveled my head in awe as it appeared to run equally as long in two different directions giving further clues to the massive size of the home.

Mrs. Bishara gave me another warm smile and a pat on the arm as she bowed and took her leave down one of the corridors. I smelled food and saw other servants in the direction she headed. I surmised that the kitchen was in that direction. Meanwhile, Okiyo knocked twice on the door directly in front of us. Not waiting for a response, he opened it and beckoned me to follow him inside.

It was a lavish office. Standing center in front of a huge wooden desk, my father stood. I froze. A million more thoughts. All my suppressed feelings. Anger. Frustration. Hurt. Love. Remembrance. All tormented me in that short span of time. I wanted to flip a desk and run to him and fall in his arms at the same time. I wanted to cry and curse him out. But no words came from my lips. My throat was too tight.

He beckoned us closer, with a clipped wave of his hand. He had an air of distinction and was at home fully dressed in a tailored suit and polished leather shoes. This man was as staunchly in charge here as he was at the studio.

I didn't move at first, but with faculties slowly restoring, I chose fight over flight. Shoulders squared, head back I stood my ground. I was not moving so he pushed away from the desk and walked to me. As he did, I allowed my eyes to roam his face before directing them to his eyes. I would not be popping to attention for this man as I'd witnessed others do. He had thirty years of explaining to do before I'd even consider pissing on him if we were on fire.

I sidestepped his hug and stuck out a hand for a handshake. My impassive face gave none of my nerves away as I simply and calmly asked, "Why am I here?"

His eyes dropped before quickly recovering. He took my hand, shaking it firmly. I turned as he regarded Okiyo who was still in the doorway. "Please give us the room," he quietly commanded.

Okiyo nodded and stepped back into the hallway. Before he closed the door, I noticed a regal woman passing by. She slowed, glaring at my father before turning her attention to me. Her cold eyes met mine briefly before she looked me up and down so fast, had I not felt her disdain, I may have missed it. As quick as she appeared, she was gone and the door was closed.

My father waved me deeper into the office to take a seat. I took the seat offered but not before raising a sarcastic brow at him. "Looks like someone is not so happy that the child you abandoned is in your home."

"Andra," he said, clearing his throat and giving a brief sardonic chuckle. Clearly taking note of my remark. Choosing to ignore it. "It's nice to finally meet you. Again."

"Umph," was the only response I could muster, mimicking his silent perusal. I wanted to yell at him. Tell him to go fuck himself— that he should have been there years ago when I needed him most. With raised brow and tucked lips, I gave him a nod of acknowledgement before taking a seat opposite him. Ready to get answers.

"Why did you abandon me?" I asked again, catching him slightly off guard. "I was only four. I was a good girl," I said matter-of-factly as if ticking off all the reasons he should have stayed. Even then, the sad little girl inside of me wondered what she could have done that was so bad her daddy would leave her. I had to hold my inner child at bay and stay calm.

He cleared his throat, choosing his words carefully. "I didn't abandon you," he began, cutting to the chase. "Your mother couldn't understand my culture and family responsibilities so she forbade me to contact you."

"So we're blaming my mother for you being a dead-beat dad?" I interjected, scoffing at his words incredulously. I squeezed my eyes shut to gain my composure before rolling them back to pin him with a disgusted look.

He pressed his lips together, looking at his hands in search of the right words. "Andra, in my culture, your culture," he said, hands spread wide as he continued, "Arranged marriages are customary here." He paused. A smile played at the corners of his mouth. It was a sad smile as if he suffered through a fleeting memory of a time long past. Starting again, he stated, "I loved your mother. So much so, I would have betrayed my family to stay there with her. With you. But fate would not have it that way."

He trained his eyes on me, smile waning. "There are things I cannot say to you because they are not mine to say, but when I met your mother all those years ago... I was a guest lecturer in her African Studies course. She was my student. It was a temporary assignment and part of my Doctorate program while I was in the US to pursue my business degree at Morehouse. It was wrong, us being together. I tried to deny my feelings for her, but I fell in love."

"You call leaving love?" I scoffed again. "You're a coward," I said, staring him down.

Undaunted, he continued. "Things happened so fast between us, that I didn't immediately tell her I was already promised to another. I was young and stupid and thought I could outsmart family commitments. When I finally told her, your mother didn't understand. She didn't take it seriously. That was my fault because neither did I."

He continued on as I studied his features and the faraway look in his eyes. I looked like him. My mother's golden tan complexion, but his nose, eyes and lips were imprinted on my features. I was busy focusing on his face when he'd said the word duty sending volts of anger up my spine.

"I was caught up between two worlds. One in which the woman I loved existed. The other where I was bound by duty," he said.

"Wasn't I your duty?" I hissed, almost coming to my feet, the hurt coiled so tightly.

"Andra, please let me finish. I pray that if you let me finish you will understand," his eyes pleaded.

I swallowed hard. But waved a hand for him to continue.

"Before long pressures to come home to run the family business had me flying back and forth between Kenya and Atlanta. I couldn't marry her when I wanted because I was only in the US on a student and temporary work visa."

He stopped again, composing himself, pain etched in his face. He continued. "Then you were born. I stayed in Atlanta as much as I could. I knew I would have to make a choice to stay and cut family ties or tell my family about you and Evelyn and refuse to marry my selected bride. Either decision would ruin my family name." He paused, again. Face now etched in shame because we both know he made neither of those choices. Looking down at his hands again, his shoulders sagged beneath the weight of his admissions of abandoning me for wealth. He sighed, again looking away taking a deep breath to still himself.

When his eyes were back on mine, his face was masked and I instinctively knew there was something he was leaving out, but I did not interrupt.

"You came along, my first born and I could not even tell my mother about you," This time when he looked away, I could feel the pain written on his face. "I made excuse after excuse after excuse to your mother about why the time was not right to bring you both home to meet your family here. Long story short, weeks became months and months became years. And just before you turned four, I was called back home. My father, your grandfather, died unexpectedly. The time I thought I had to convince him to get me out of the arranged marriage had passed."

He stopped, straightening the sleeve of his jacket as I watched the battle of emotions waging war on his face. I knew that the act of fixing his clothes was a tethering act to keep himself from falling apart. I saw loss in his eyes as he continued on.

"When I went home for his funeral, I found that the family business was suffering financially. Had been for a while and was the main reason my marriage was arranged. I was promised to the daughter of the then Chief, also the major investor in my father's business as payment for the debt." My father's eyes were on me now, imploring me to understand. "If I didn't marry his daughter he threatened to take my father's business, leaving my mother and all of my siblings destitute. I came home to your mother to explain but she didn't understand and rightfully so. The moment she found out I was married, she made me leave and forbade me to contact you or her ever again. I left that morning without being able to tell you goodbye and I have ached every day since."

My father walked away from his desk to a window. He stood there, staring out for a moment, shoulders drooped, making him appear years older than the regal man that greeted me upon entering this office. He placed a hand on the window as if touching a distant place in the past.

Without looking at me, he continued. "I called every day until Evelyn finally changed the number. Initially, I sent money to cover your monthly expenses by means of cashier's checks. All returned to sender. She had moved you both to a new home. Completely shutting me out. Years later, I brought on Okiyo as head of my family security. He used his connections and found you. At first, I kept my distance— well sort of, but have kept a close eye on you ever since." At that he turned to me, eyes beseeching.

"Wha— what? What do you mean you've watched over me ever since? That doesn't make sense. If you knew where I was, why not pick up the phone? Send an email, something. The internet has been in existence all my life," I yelled.

What the fuck did he mean he knew where I was and how to contact me for years and he didn't? This time the tears overflowed.

"I cried for months, years missing you so bad it hurt. I grew up trying to be you! Never allowed a man to get close to me because of YOU," My rising voice broke, as I choked on the sob caught in my throat.

When I looked up at him, expecting an answer, he bowed his head over praying fingers. He shifted nervously in his position by the window then in almost a whisper, he calmly said, "I have talked to you and your dear friend Kobe at least once a week for the better part of 10 years now."

When my face crumbled in confusion, he continued, voice stronger now. "Andra," he paused again, "I am Daddy_ B_ Right."

"No," I stood, grabbing my chest, stepping back in astonishment. "That's not possible. How is that even possible?" I laughed crazily as all the clues began playing back. The out of nowhere change in the filming line up to go to the Maasai Mara. Okiyo knew details about me; about Kobe when they'd never met each other. Two deals that couldn't be refused by me or my best friend ultimately getting me to come to Kenya. None of it was a coincidence. An anonymous venture capitalist my ass.

"What the fuck is going on?" I questioned, still shaking my head in disbelief. All these years he'd been watching me? Talking to me? Forging online relationships with my best friend? Kobe damn near worshiped this man. Hell, so did I.

He'd embedded himself in my life under the guise of a fake fucking profile on Instagram. *Nooo. No. No. No. No. Noooo. No. No. No.* I paced around the room, hands up and clasped behind my head as the absurdity of it all sank in. *I'd been catfished by Chief fucking Daddy.* I had fawned over his age-appropriate photo, calling him Zaddy even. *Ew.*

I looked at him, my eyes wide with questions but the words stuck in my throat. He nodded silently as if he knew what I was thinking and opened his mouth to say something, but nothing came out. And just as my knees gave out, he rushed to me, wrapping me in his arms as I crumpled. He guided me down to the floor, cradling me back and forth as I fell apart in his arms. I don't know how long we stayed there on the floor in his office but he didn't let go. He held me in his arms long past my sobs growing silent.

He broke the embrace first, pushing me back at arm's length soaking in my face as a father who hadn't seen his oldest daughter in person since she was four years old would. "*Ma'baby* gourd," he sighed. He had been crying too. The crystal glint of an unchecked tear hovered in the corner of his eye. "Please forgive me."

I wasn't sure if I could. But I also couldn't walk away.

We had so much to talk about. My father asked and I'd agreed to spend the night at his estate, which he'd adamantly referred to as my home. I had just met the man officially so I wasn't quite sure how to feel about referring to his space as home.

After sharing that he'd been waiting for this day for so long he summoned Mrs. Bishara to show me to one of the guest suites so that I could relax a little while before dinner. I took him up on the offer because I indeed was still reeling from our emotionally charged first meeting.

I had not been in the beautiful, well-appointed room for more than 10 minutes before my cell phone scattered across the side table as an incoming call blared and vibrated loudly. Kobe's face appeared on the screen. I sat up quickly and grabbed the phone answering it before it could roll to voicemail.

"Kobe," I shouted into the receiver, so glad to see his face. "I am so sorry."

"Naw, *baby'gyul*. I'm the one who should be sorry. Shouldn't have made moves with another brand without chopping it up with you first."

"Umm," I stammered... Dismissing the thought of Carmel and that stupid post. A wave of jealousy washed over me but I tamped it down because the need for my friend outweighed everything right now. And with everything else that transpired, now wasn't the time for that. "No. Kobe, I was a jerk to you. I've been distant and busy... *Fuck*," I croaked, Swallowing a sob, fresh tears threatening to spill. "Kobe..." I attempted again and fell apart.

"Yo Andra. What's wrong?" He questioned, on high alert at my cry. I wasn't a crier and aside from attitude and anger, I skirted emotions, tucking them deep inside. He knew this. Knew me. And even though I'd been distant and a straight up bitch to him, Kobe was always on my team. I had always taken that for granted. I had always taken him for granted. Even now, not even knowing why, he would scorch the earth over my tears. I owed him so much more than an apology. "Anj? Talk to me."

Before I could even temper the words, they spilled from my lips.

"I found him, Kobe."

"Found who?"

"Daddy_B_Right."

"Daddy_B_Right? Andra, what are you talking about? Why are you cry—"

"Daddy be right! Daddy of Andra Bainswright. Daddy_B_Right is my father!"

Chapter 19 – Andra

♥

I AWOKE WITH A start from the light rapping at the door. Still a bit groggy from my sleep, I remembered laying across the bed still reeling from the events of the day but fortified by the call from Kobe. I'd been emotionally drained and must have dozed off.

It felt as though I had only closed my eyes for a moment. But it was more like hours. It was nearly dark outside. Mrs. Bishara had poked her head in to announce that dinner would be served in twenty minutes.

"Andra, gyul," she said, reminding me of how Kobe referred to me when he was either excited about something or irritated with me. "I have stocked the water closet with washcloths, towels, and soap. And you have a small bag of your belongings, there," she pointed at the small leather overnight bag on the dresser across the room. I followed her eyes curiously.

"A bag with my belongings?" I looked back at her questioning.

"Oh yes. Your father sent Okiyo to grab you a few things from your condo. I brought them while you slept. Come now, wash up for dinner." She waved me towards the bathroom. "I will wait outside to escort you down to the formal dining room."

Alone again, I inspected the contents of the small bag, impressed that Okiyo was so thorough in grabbing the things I'd need. My toiletries, small makeup bag, toothbrush and toothpaste were all here.

There were a couple of changes of clothes, matching shoes, and... *No the fuck he didn't!* This man even packed my underwear... matching sets too. Now this was a bit beyond efficient. My cheeks and ears pricked with heat as I thought of him rummaging through my undergarments to find the matching bra and panties. Embarrassed, yes, but I had to stifle a giggle as I thought of him holding them delicately up one by one to place them gingerly into my bag. That damned proper gentleman, Okiyo.

I shook my head as I grabbed the simple indigo colored Ivy Park midi spandex dress he'd chosen along with a bright pair of strappy, heeled sandals. Deciding against a shower, I dashed to the bathroom to rid myself of the crumpled clothes I'd arrived and slept in. Then I hit all my spicy parts with soap and fresh water from the sink and dressed. Fresh faced, save for a light dusting of bronzer, lip gloss and mascara, I was ready to eat.

Once at the ornate double doors of the dining room, Mrs. Bishara turned to give me a rampart smile, then pushed them open announcing me as if we were at the grand entrance of a presidential palace. *Damn.* This was a bit much for dinner at the house, I thought before entering behind her into the elegant white room.

Bright red, blue, purple, and pink floral arrangements adorned the credenza along the wall. Minimalist abstract paintings in the same colors lined the walls adding to the Instagram worthy vibe of the room. A huge crystal chandelier was centered above the table and actual candles burned in huge candelabras at its center. I had to force my mouth closed as I gawked at the sheer over the top-ness of it all.

Had I not realized that several people including my father and Okiyo were already seated at the expansive table, I might have been compelled to run and get my phone to take pictures. Feeling the weight of eight pairs of eyes staring at me, I froze.

I tugged at my dress to find something to do with my hands under the scrutiny of the two women sitting at the table. They stared hard. The older one, the same woman in the doorway of my father's office from earlier, openly looked me up and down. This time, her cold aloofness prickled my nerves a bit. The younger of the two ladies, clearly related to the older lady, also looked me up and down. Her appraisal was bolder. She openly stared then pursed her lips before slowly sucking her teeth and turning back to the conversation she'd been having with the older woman. *Had this bitch just dismissed me?*

Seeing my slight discomfort, my father rose from his position at the head of the table, clearing his throat before saying, "Andra, come on in and join us." He reached out his right hand beckoning me to the end of what had to be a 20-foot table, pulling out the chair to his right side between he and Okiyo, who stood as well, bowing his head, and offering a brief but friendly smile of welcome. I almost curtsied at his ass like some *Bridgerton* shit.

"Everyone, this is Andra," my father continued. "Andra, I want to introduce you to Kwamboka, Kwam as everyone calls her, my wife—"

"Mrs. Baijan will do," the woman interjected.

My father looked down at her, his irritation barely bridled, before turning his attention to the younger Cruella Deville. "And this is Makena, your younger sister."

And there it was. I immediately understood and was almost sympathetic to both of the ladies. Apparently they knew about me, the bastard child from America. That much was obvious. Whether they knew I would be here today, was another whole question.

"Wow. Sister?" I said, a shocked smile plastered on my face, truly not expecting that one. All these years of pining for my daddy, I never placed other siblings into the equation. "It's a pleasure to meet you both. Mrs. Baijan. Sister." I stammered; quite sure the sentiment was not mutual.

No response from, *Qualm*, Kwam or whatever the fuck her name was. A twirl of fingers in my direction from the younger was the closest thing to a greeting I'd be getting from either of the two, before they went back to a hushed conversation with each other, all but dismissing me.

I took my seat, noticing the squinted look Okiyo gave me as if to communicate that I was safe here. I smiled briefly at him; glad I wasn't in this lion's den on my own.

My father took his seat once I was neatly tucked into mine. He cleared his throat before directing his attention to his wife to break up her cliquish conversation with her daughter. Their obvious intention was to shut everyone else at the table out. She continued to ignore him, turning her body even more toward Makena. This time raising her voice as she asked, "Dear, did you get the Givenchy dress that I had sent over for you to try on?"

My sister responded equally loud, "Yes. It was exactly what I was looking for. You know I can't be running around the office party next week looking..." she paused, slightly tipping her head in my direction. "Common."

Ouch. Okay Bitch, I get it. You don't want me here. I took a deep breath to shake off the attitude that if unchecked may have me flipping this table on this little cunt.

She smiled sweetly then turned her attention fully to me as though a thought had occurred. "Andra, that is a cute little number you're wearing. It's giving," she raised her eyes in the air, placing a finger at the corner of her mouth as she contemplated my outfit, "Rap guys girlfriend."

"Andra, you look very nice—" my father began to cover up the rudeness of his youngest child, but I cut him off.

"I guess you could say, it's the most famous rapper's wife's design." I looked down at my simple dress, feeling underdressed in luxury athleisure for this crowd , but wasn't going to let this childish bitch know that. "It's a custom dress that was given to me from the Ivy Park collection through our very lucrative brand sponsorship with them." My head angled slightly to the side, giving her pettiness right back before leveling my eyes on her in a steady unblinking glare. She had the nerve to wriggle her pug little nose and turn her attention back to Queen Petty, Qualm.

Okiyo grabbed his glass of wine, tipping it to his mouth to quickly cover the chuckle that escaped with a cough. His raised brow, quirked in my direction, a tickled gleam in his eye. He dipped his head appreciatively in silent applause for standing up for myself against these formidable ladies.

The atmosphere continued to brighten after I put the petty ones on notice that I was not going to be intimidated by them when Mrs. Bishara and two more servers entered and placed baskets of fresh *chapati*, flat bread, on the table, pinching Okiyo's cheek and winking at me as she did.

And with that, dinner was served. Aside from the occasional snide remark from the younger of the two and the cold regard of the older, dinner went off without a hitch.

After the last course was served, Okiyo and my father were discussing business and the two mean girls were still ignoring the rest of the table as they continued on about every detail of the same damn Givenchy dress.

I took the opportunity to explore the beautiful space. The back wall of the dining room was made of floor to ceiling windows and double french doors. I could see the glowing blue light of the pool beyond. Its sparkling beauty lighting the night, beckoned me out the doors. I stood beside the cool blue waters, studying the well-manicured, lit gardens beyond.

It was peaceful out here. The night air was a bit warm but it felt good to get away from the cold regard from the dining room. The peace was short lived as I heard her heels approaching before I saw which of the two women it could be. Neither option was any that I would want company from.

"Couldn't stand the heat, I see." Makena's voice cut through the night. I fought to not turn around and look her up and down before asking her meaning. I had to breathe deeply and relax my stiff shoulders. I mean on the one hand, I'd feel some kind of way too if a virtual stranger showed up to my Daddy's home and was introduced as my sister, too. On the other hand, I was a victim here as well and we were going to have to come to some amicable understanding. I was the older sister, so I decided to extend the olive branch.

I turned slowly with a smile on my face. "Actually, it was a little chilly inside," I paused, knowing she'd catch my reference to her and her mother. "I'm glad for the lingering warmth of the evening out here. It's beautiful by the way."

Makena said nothing, just sidled closer to stand beside me. She stood a few inches taller, made obvious as she turned her head glancing down at me. She crossed her arms then turned to face me dead on.

Unphased, I squared and turned to her. We stood face to face, mere inches apart as I continued. "So, what do you like to do for fun?" My words were light, but there was nothing light in the air between us. I hoped she'd take the olive branch and soften a bit. Not a chance.

My half-sister gave me a withering look. "Fun?" She sniffed. "There is nothing about my father's bastard child showing up and being paraded around town, given TV deals and the like that would be considered fun. Hopefully this little farse won't last. Ask him for money already and fuck right off back to America."

I blinked rapidly, stunned by her flat-out attack. As I shuffled uncomfortably, she sidled in closer, "What?" she said, her voice cold and sharp as a knife. "Did you think that the fake ass smile you just graced me with would melt me and have me sniffing your skirt tail in hopes you'd be my older sister?" She laughed out loud this time, tossing her head back at the absurdity of the idea. "You think you can come here, into Daddy's house - our house - and pretend like none of this is weird? That we're some kind of family?" She laughed again, bitterly. "Think again."

Well so much for that olive branch. Her words actually stung a bit, but I'd be damned if this brat would have me shook. Not when I didn't ask to be here. I didn't ask for the fucking tv deal and Kobe damned sure hadn't asked for that restaurant. If this little bitch thought that she was going to chump me off, she had another fucking thing coming.

I held my ground, spreading an even sweeter smile on my face before responding. "No, I don't expect anything from you," I replied softly, "but I think I'm going to stick around a little longer, to get to know my Daddy." I made sure to let the word drip from my lips like honey.

Lifting a demure finger to the corner of my mouth as if in thought, I regarded her with a bored side glance before finishing, "I hope that won't make you and your mother too uncomfortable." I turned and left her standing where she was, paying her zero ounces more of my attention. I chuckled loudly, not breaking my stride when I heard her huff out a seething, "Bitch" to my back.

Chapter 20 –Kobe

♥

A FEW DAYS HAD passed since the break-in at the restaurant. The studio was well aware of what had happened and just like before, seemed to be unphased about the delay in our opening schedule that this would cause.

These mofos seriously acted like money was no object. Being the stickler that I was, Gastrafrique would operate and my kitchen would run as efficiently as possible. I charged forward, to first work with the security company to have them replace the entire security system from the sensors to the wall panels. Everything. I know I armed that system. Their shit had to be faulty.

I also worked with the insurance company and was assured that all the equipment that was stolen was properly insured and they had already cut a check so that I could reorder everything. I was able to negotiate delivery for the new equipment within the next two weeks. It hadn't yet been installed. In essence, the grand opening would only be delayed by two weeks. Possibly less if every-thing fell into place as planned.

And things were looking up. The construction company who was doing the buildout for the restaurant was actually ahead of schedule and only needed to install the heavy equip-ment on order in the massive kitchen. That allowed the interior designer and her team to get a head start on pulling the beau-tiful design together. That meant that Gastrafrique would be ready to open in less than six weeks.

It was time to start pushing hard on hiring the remaining open positions. I was waiting for my mother to show up so that we could make the final touches to the menu today. I had a couple of hours to schedule a few interviews for waitstaff, sous chefs, and a restaurant manager. I'd already interviewed and hired two bartenders and the main manager. Both would be in later today to begin preliminary training.

I was hanging up a call when Carmel\ walked into my office. I stood to give her a hug when my cell phone rang in my pocket. I wrapped one arm around her waist as I pulled it out, noticing the Kenyan country code. It was the same code that came up from Andra's new phone number, but it wasn't hers. Thinking it was strange, I placed a quick peck on Carmel's cheek. "Hey babe." I said. "Give me a second to take this call."

"Sure." She said, stepping back to give a bit of privacy but not leaving my office. It was cool. I didn't know this number and had nothing to hide from her anyway.

"Hello," I greeted.

"Mr. Abara," the deep voice on the other end, greeted in absolute certainty that he'd reached the right person. "This is Leboo Baijan." The caller paused, then cleared his throat. "You may know me as Daddy_B_Right."

I stammered in shock at the name provided by the caller. Andra had told me on our last call about the revelation that her father had made about being the super fan that had followed Gastrafrique for the better half of ten years. I was shocked when she told me. I was even more shocked at the announcement the man on the other end of the call had just made. The caller cleared his throat again, sounding a bit embarrassed.

"I am sure Andra has made you aware of the circumstances of our meeting."

"Um... Yeah. She mentioned it," I responded hesitantly, not quite knowing what else to say to him about the circumstances of their meeting as he put it. Andra and I had caught up with each other just the other day in what seemed like the first real time since she'd been gone and here he was calling me. I wasn't sure how I fit into this shit show.

"Kobe. I want to apologize for my deceitful actions over the years, but I hope you do understand that I only had the best interest of my daughter in mind. It was the only way I could build a relationship with her and, uh..." His voice trailed off as he seemingly searched for more words.

I was rendered silent. What was I supposed to say to this man? Didn't quite blame him for wanting to be in his daughter's life, but that was some bitch shit to keep his identity hidden all these years. I mean, I didn't know the circumstances of why he did that. Wasn't sure there was anything he could say to make me understand.

I mean, Andra meant the world to me and I'd seen how she was affected by not having him in her life. Had watched her try to keep her tears at bay when we were school kids and my dad and everybody else's dad was in their lives. While she barely had her mother, no shade to Ms. Evelyn, but she was caught up in the rat race as a single mother, focused on busting her ass to take care of Andra instead of going on school field trips. I didn't know what he wanted me to say. So I said nothing.

As if to read my mind, Andra's father continued. "Let me start again. For years, I have followed my daughter and you, Kobe on Gastrafrique." He paused, clearing his throat again before chuckling wryly. "I needn't bore you with the details that I'm sure you already know." His voice trailed off again, thoughtfully. "Just know that I had to be in my daughter's life in some way and this was the best way that made sense at the time."

"I can understand that, but she needed you," I said simply. Not an accusation. Just facts. The words held a space between us.

Taking the leap over the space that could have ended the call, Leboo took a deep breath and continued. "Over the years of following the two of you, I realized that you were a Godsend, Kobe. Without question, you protected and covered *ma'baby* when I couldn't. Didn't as her father. I cannot make up for the time I wasn't in my daughter's life. But knowing she had you to watch over her, made it a little easier to bear that I might never get to know my oldest child. For that I owe you my gratitude."

Carmel stood on the other side of my office, eyes locked on mine as she witnessed the smattering of shock, confusion, and eventual understanding of what the man was saying cross my face. I hunched my shoulders in her direction to let her know that I would explain when I finished. I turned my attention back to the call.

Leboo took a deep breath on the other end, redirecting us to the purpose of his call. "At any rate, I understand that there was a mishap that you've been dealing with at the restaurant."

I was taken aback on how he knew this. I hadn't even shared the break in with Andra, not wanting to say much while she was dealing with... all this. Meeting her dad. Then almost clapping myself across the head, I remembered he was the anonymous venture capitalist. Of course he would know. It was his money funding both the tv show and the restaurant.

"I also hear that under your capable thumb, the launch is only slightly delayed," he chuckled. "Kobe, I want to say how proud I am of you. As I knew my daughter was in good hands with you all these years, so too did I know that you would do a phenomenal job of launching the restaurant. Again, I have to apologize for breaking up the dynamic duo. But I'm sure you understand that I had to lure Andra here some kind of way without giving up my identity. Ahh, and the tv show is rapping soon too. I think it's high time to bring you two back together again. We are holding a party in honor of the successful completion of the tv show and I want you to be here. It would be a total surprise to Andra, so I implore you not to say anything."

"Of course I will be there. Anything for her. When is it?" I asked, noticing the flash of anger in Carmel's narrowed eyes. I was getting tired of that shit; I thought as I repeated the dates back to Andra's dad to make sure I got them right as I wrote the information on my desk calendar. "Yep, that's in a few weeks. I'll be there Daddy_B_Right. I mean Mr. *err*."

"Call me Leboo, son." He said chuckling before ending the call.

When I hung up the phone, I rounded on Carmel, locking eyes before she tried to look away. "That was Andra's dad." I studied her intently for that same flicker. She stared back, barely suppressing her irritation. I didn't care. Her mood shifts at the sheer mention of Andra's name would stop and I let her know just that before calmly filling her in on the details Leboo had just shared with me. "Looks like I'm heading to Kenya for the big Gastrafrique wrap party. It's going to be a big celebration for Andra –"

Obviously not taking me seriously, Carmel kept right on with the slick shit about Andra. Cutting me off she threw her hands up, sarcastically saying, "Right. The world stops for Andra. So much for the plans I was coming to share with you."

"Hey," I almost shouted, making her jump. I really didn't care but I asked anyway. "What plans?" Before she could answer, my mother joined us in the office, gladly interrupting what was surely about to be an argument.

"Hello *ma'Baby*!" She sang, all bright eyed and bushy tailed. That is until she noticed Carmel's bright red cheeks, flared nostrils, and tight brow. To which my mother's smile faded as she regarded Carmel with a head to toe up down with her eyes, "Carmel." She greeted.

Blowing out a breath of exasperation, Carmel turned to the door to leave, tossing a quick, "Mrs. Abara, good to see you. Kobe, I guess we can talk about this later," Over her shoulder. In my opinion, there was nothing left for us to talk about. She left in a huff leaving my mother ping ponging her head back and forth between the two of us. All I could think was good riddance.

My mother chortled at Carmel's retreating back. "Do tell. What is wrong with her?"

I shrugged, deciding to let it go and tell my mother about the phone call I'd just received and the trip to Kenya I would be taking in a few weeks.

My mother was as shocked as I was to learn the wild shit about who Andra's daddy was.

Chapter 21 – Andra

♥

OKIYO ESCORTED ME TO the event. Not as my transportation liaison, but as my plus one, 'aka' my bodyguard. Deke pulled up directly in front of the red carpet at the entrance of the venue. Okiyo came around to open my door and offered his arm to assist me out of the back seat.

As soon as we took the first step on the carpet, cameras began flashing. The show hadn't even premiered yet and the media crews from local Kenyan and other outlets were there in force. It was a star-studded event. The glitz and the glam of it all made me feel like I had arrived. *I wish Kobe was here for this.*

My father tried to prepare me for the spectacle, but I had no idea it would be like this. I was far from a star or household name, but by the constant calls from the media, "Ms. Bainswright," "over here," "look this way," I felt like a star at the Grammys.

I acted the part. Taking photo after photo. Mostly alone while Okiyo played the background. I had to admit he was sharp. A proper British gentleman in a three-piece tailored suit and pocket watch to boot. It was a black-tie affair and everyone looked amazing, but per usual, his style was elevated.

My dress, though not couture, rivaled any designer dress in the building and looked better than any of the four that my father had sent to my condo along with a personal stylist to try them on.

The party was held just beyond the lobby in the hotel gardens. The red carpet was a masterpiece, splashed with bursts of floral colors that escorted us from the lobby all the way along the illuminated garden paths.

By the time we arrived, the wrap party was already in full swing. There was the hum of animated conversation, the chime of clinking glasses, the buzz of a crowd enjoying the night.

White gloved servers in tuxes zipped through the crowd serving champagne and hors d'oeuvres. I recognized personalities from a few of the popular Food Network and HG TV shows in attendance along with other well-known entertainers from music and television.

I was totally fangirling on Okiyo's arm when I spotted a popular Afrobeats singer that both Kobe and I loved. Before long, I spotted my father. He waved us over.

"Andra," he called, "I'd like to introduce you to David Berkowitz, the head of the LA studio. He's been instrumental in getting the show greenlit. Also, he provided all of the support necessary for the Atlanta team to get the restaurant up and running."

I reached out my hand to shake his. "It's a pleasure to meet you Ms. Bainswright," David said. Grabbing my hand and shaking it firmly. "I've had the privilege of seeing a bit of the preliminary footage for the show and I'm fairly confident in saying, I think, we've got a hit on our hands."

"Wow," I smiled back and forth between him and my father. "That is amazing. Most days I wasn't sure if all the footage would end up on the cutting room floor." We all laughed at my quip. Me, a nervous giggle because I'm sure Kayla, who I'd spied while walking over, would have agreed with how bad I was when we first started filming.

Sobering, my father softened his gaze and encouragingly stated, "My dear, it was precisely when you stopped trying to act that we knew the show was going to be a success."

Mr. Berkowitz nodded his head in agreement with my father and asked, "Are you ready for the show to air in just under a month?"

"A month?" I stammered surprised. "I know we finished filming and everything is in post production. But I had no idea we'd air that quickly."

Both men chuckled again, this time at my novice understanding of modern tv production.

"Ah the marvels of technology, my dear. What used to take a long time now only takes a matter of days with the right team. And I'd say we picked the right team."

I stood with my father and Mr. Berkowitz for a few more moments discussing the promo tour and marketing strategy for the show. Even though it wasn't widely known that I was his daughter. Hell, I wasn't sure anyone knew outside of my immediate family, including Kobe and Okiyo. Nonetheless, I was proud to be his daughter. Basking in that sentiment was short lived because out of the corner of my eye I could see Kwam throwing nasty looks in mine and my father's direction.

She was sitting at one of the white, linen covered tables. From the look of it, she was quite put out that my father was publicly engaging with me. Unbridled distaste simmered in her eyes as she tossed back an entire glass of champagne she'd been nursing. I had to fight not to send a nasty smirk in her direction.

Instead, I graciously excused myself from the conversation with my father and Mr. Berkowitz so I could mingle.

I had to admit the black-tie affair was lit. Famsi, the same Afrobeats star I'd seen earlier had taken the stage and many in the crowd were hiking up dresses and attempting not to scuff their polished shoes to cut a rug.

The atmosphere was so festive that my nerves at the thought of having to stand up in front of all these folks to give a speech later were now nonexistent. I pulled out my phone and decided to live stream some of the event on Gastrafrique's Instagram.

Before hitting the live button on my phone, I noticed that Kobe was already live streaming on our account. I'd only caught the tail end of his before he signed off. From what I could tell, he'd been streaming from a hotel room. He seemed to be getting dressed to go out, I assumed on a date or something from the snippet of his outfit I could see before the screen went black. I couldn't help the pang of jealousy I'd felt at the thought of him going on another date with Carmel.

I shrugged it off, then clicked to start the live stream again, undoubtedly giving our fans a surprise of two streams back-to-back. I turned the camera on myself and threw on a dazzling smile, ensuring the span of the festive party was in full view of the camera. Within three minutes of my live starting, 5000 viewers were tuned in.

"Hello, you African Food Freaks! It's your girl Andra filming live from Nairobi, Kenya! I know it's been awhile but I had to bring y'all to the party. You guys see this!" I said giddily, panning the camera around so my viewers could see festivities. I flipped the camera back around to face me while chanting, "Ain't no party like a Gastrafrique party cause a Gastrafrique party don't stop!"

The chat went wild. Hearts, Kenyan flags, and thumbs up emojis flew across the screen. I continued, "Your girl just wanted to come on here and say thank you to all for standing by me and Kobe as we stepped away a little to do big things. For that, I'm bringing y'all all the way into the action." I panned my phone around again, this time so they could get a good view of the stage. "We've got Famsi on stage!" I squealed excitedly as I handed my phone to a waiter walking by so he could capture me doing a little *Xanku* shimmy and a two step to the heavy baseline of the Billboard charting song. Afrobeats was so mainstream now, everyone knew the song. After a few minutes of partying, I retrieved my phone and turned it back on me. I continued to amp the audience. "Y'all don't mind me. I'm just a little *litty* from this champagne." I held up the flute I'd grabbed from the tray of the passing waiter. "And I have a big secret to tell." I made a grand gesture of looking around to see if anyone near me was in hearing distance as I pulled my phone near my face and whisper yelled into the speaker, "The Gastrafrique TV show has wrapped and it's gonna be released in less than a month!" The screen exploded with emojis as I jumped up and down giddy at their surprised reaction. Before signing off the live, I shared that we had a few more announcements that would be made soon and that I couldn't wait until Kobe and I were back on camera together again.

I threw up a peace sign before clicking end on the live. It had been forever since I interacted with our fans. I missed them so much but I missed me and Kobe in front of them even more.

Chapter 22 – Andra

♥

NOT LONG AFTER I ended the live, the music quieted and the emcee spoke into the mic to get everyone's attention. The room came to a hush and everybody including myself was focused on the stage. He began, "Welcome everyone as we gather to celebrate the wrap of the Gastrafrique show. Everyone, please give a round of applause to Mr. Leboo Baijan."

The room went up in a roar of applause as my father made his way to ascend the stairs, taking center stage. He reached for the mic and the crowd exploded in applause again. It was still very new to me just how well known and important my father was in the entertainment industry.

He began speaking and the room went quiet. "I want to thank all of you for coming out to celebrate the cast and crew and all who were involved in the making of the Gastrafrique TV show." He paused to let the applause die down again. "Many of you thought I was crazy when I pitched the idea for both the Gastrafrique TV show and restaurant based solely on two kids out of Atlanta GA who simply loved African food and culture. The bigwigs over at the Food Network were a lot less apprehensive when I offered to pay for both using no studio dollars."

The crowd burst out laughing at his joke. My father was a charismatic speaker and had the audience eating from the palm of his hand.

He continued, "I knew in my core that both the restaurant and TV show would be a success. So much so, I was willing to bet my reputation on it. I'm sure you're all wondering why I would take such a risky endeavor," he looked shrewdly out at the audience as he gave space for everyone to quietly contemplate his question. "Well, I'll let you in on a secret. I knew the show would be a success because one half of the dynamic duo that makes-up Gastrafrique is my daughter." *Mic drop.*

From the sound of collective gasp from the audience, I could tell that what my father had just revealed was scandal making news amongst these circles. He had all but announced to the entire cast, crew, studio execs, and his peers in the presence of his wife and legitimate daughter that he had fathered a child out of wedlock.

With an unwavering gaze and a steadfast voice, my father asserted his belief. "Andra Bainswright, my eldest child, was not just born into greatness but also forged it. She is of my flesh, my spirit, and my tenacity. Today's announcement may have caught many of you off guard, but I assure you, this has been a decade in the making."

"I have watched, with paternal pride and a businessman's scrutiny, as she and her partner Kobe built a culinary empire. Their passion for African cuisine wasn't just a hobby—it was a mission. A mission to bring the authentic flavors of Africa to the forefront of global gastronomy. The likes of fufu, ugali, mandazi, and countless other treasures from the African continent aren't just footnotes in their journey; they're the stars."

"Theirs was a labor of love, but also a strategic endeavor. They took our heritage, our family recipes, and they built a platform around it. Not just any platform—a highly lucrative social media engine that has been fueled by their relentless drive and innovation."

"They have made African cuisine not just recognizable, but aspirational. They've made our food, our culture, a household name. A cuisine that stands shoulder to shoulder with the greatest culinary traditions of the world."

He paused for effect, letting his words sink in. "I didn't just bet on a TV show and a restaurant. I bet on two visionaries who dared to dream, dared to challenge the status quo. I bet on Andra and Kobe. And today, we all stand here, reaping the rewards of their success, their vision. And that, ladies and gentlemen, is why

I staked my reputation, my resources on them. Because I believed in them, and I always will."

As my father beamed at me across the audience, the lights in the garden dimmed and a spotlight was trained on me. "I was fanning the tears that were slowly forming from the depth of his words, feeling every bit of the legitimacy my father just gave me. I had to blink back the tears that threatened to spoil my makeup.

"As I stand here, I must acknowledge the remarkable contribution of Kobe Abara," my father resumed, his voice echoing through the hushed hall. "Kobe, who is not just the other half of the Gastrafrique brand, but also my daughter's closest confidante and friend."

"He stepped in where I fell short. He ensured Andra's success, safety, and well-being when I was absent. His loyalty and commitment to my daughter are beyond what any father could ask for. For this, I owe him the deepest gratitude."

Emotion filled my father's eyes as he gestured towards the empty space beside him. "Now, I invite my daughter, Andra, to join me on stage along with a special guest—without whom none of this would have been possible."

A second spotlight flickered on, illuminating the vacant spot next to my father. The anticipation in the room was palpable. Like everyone else, I was eager to see who this esteemed guest was.

I slowly started moving towards the stage, my every movement tracked by the overhead spotlight. I stopped, seeing first the highly polished shoes that stepped into the light. His stance was familiar to me. My gaze moved up to his hands, slowly making their way to the black silk lapels of his white tuxedo jacket. My breath caught in my throat as all that I knew of my heart and home came into crystal clear vision. I snatched the Jimmy Choos from my feet, clutching them firmly as I ran to the front of the room taking the stairs two at a time and threw myself into Kobe's arms.

Tears were freely running down my cheeks, now. Makeup be damned. My lifeline, my best friend was here. It was at that moment I knew the speech I'd written at my father's request for this occasion would be dedicated to Kobe, the scrawny kid from 7th grade who smiled at me as I winked at him while being drug off to the principal's office.

We stayed in that embrace for what felt like eons. Save for the raucous applause, it felt like Kobe and I were the only people in the garden. He held me tight and I clung to him as though my life depended on it.

When he finally released me, his hand sought out mine and raised the mic to his lips, "Andra, everybody!" Kissing me on the cheek, he handed me the microphone and stepped out of the spotlight.

Kobe's presence calmed me. The words I' d written and fretted about memorizing were not needed. Instead of looking at the audience I turned and looked directly at him.

"Gastrafrique is the dream of two African American kids from two sides of the African continent who literally bonded over *fufu*," I giggled, playing off the words, my father had just said. I gestured at Kobe as I continued, "It all started in your mama's kitchen in NW Atlanta.," I paused, reflecting back on that time.

"To be honest what we started wasn't about the food. We were just two misfit kids in a world that didn't see us. But we saw each other. And within each other, we found a place to belong."

I turned my gaze to my father, offering him a forgiving smile "I grew up feeling abandoned and misunderstood. But never alone. This man right here," I nodded appreciatively in Kobe's direction, "Invited me into his home, into his family, into his heart and showed me what it was to be a part of something bigger than me."

I turned to face the audience full on. "A lot of people never find something like what Kobe has given me. His mother taught us how to cook traditional West African food. Kobe taught me how to appreciate it and savor it." My voice was trembling with emotion. "That," I said, splaying my hands wide, "Is the essence of Gastrafrique. It's that essence of having a place to belong that brought 5 million followers and counting, a TV show and restaurant. Well that and my daddy's deep pockets," I paused, laughing wryly along with the audience.

I reached for Kobe's hand again and looked into his eyes and finished, "We did it best friend." He pulled me into a deep hug again and the room exploded in applause.

As soon as we were off the stage and had a bit of privacy, I rounded on Kobe, clasping his cheeks between my palms, "How did y'all pull this off?" I asked   in awe. "I saw a bit of your live on IG," I smiled ruefully, as the words tumbled out of my mouth. "I thought you were about to go on a date. With Carmel." I looked away hoping he didn't see the hurt that the thought had caused.

Kobe grabbed my chin, gently pulling my eyes back to his. "You don't have to worry about Carmel," he said softly. "It didn't work out. Apparently," he said, furrowing his brow in mock contemplation, "I'm so far up Andra's ass, I wouldn't spot Miss Right if she were doing the dougie on roller skates right in front of me." His face remained impressively serious, while I let slip a surprised chuckle, placing a hand over my mouth, as the slow contagious laugh spilled out.

Kobe's face crumbled in laughter too. "Did she really say that?" I asked, sobering a bit, not sure how he truly felt about Carmel.

"She did," Kobe took a deep breath recovering from the mirth in the situation, turning more serious, "Right before I agreed with her. I have never had eyes for another wom—"

My sister and her boyfriend idled up, interrupting the words Kobe was about to say. The boyfriend was indeed as ugly as Mrs. Bashara had conspiratorially described him to be as we shared a laugh that first night I'd stayed at my father's home. Apparently he was a big fan of Gastrafrique and to Mackena's dismay, he let Kobe know it.

"My man," he said, all but fanboying over Kobe, "I've been following Gastrafrique for years." He reached Kobe's hand, pumping it vigorously.

I stood by amused while the boyfriend asked Kobe a billion questions about his favorite Michelin star restaurants. In the meantime, I noticed my sister smiling a little too hard at Kobe. He'd seen it too and offered me an amused wink at the audacity of her giving him the eye while her boyfriend was busy *bromancing* him at the same time.

I hid a giggle at Mackena's eye roll at her boyfriend who'd totally Bogarted the conversation. He'd probably thwarted her opportunity to say something slick. I winked back at Kobe and mouthed, "We can finish our conversation later."

Out loud, I cleared my throat, "I'm going to run to the ladies room to powder my nose." I looked at McKenna, brow raised to see if she might want to join, shrugging my shoulders and taking leave when she offered a bland look in my direction.

I saw a sign leading into the hotel from the garden and thought the bathrooms would be there. They were on the other side of a large fountain that graced the center of the hallway. The fountain was stunning, with its graceful arcs and shimmering spray that glistened under the overhead lights. I admired it for a moment before attempting to navigate around it to the bathrooms on the other side. Still on a high from Kobe being here mixed with my awe at the gorgeous wall of water, I didn't see her until I collided with Kwam, my stepmother.

She grabbed me roughly, her grip tight and unforgiving as she halted me from walking past her. Her fingers dug painfully into my bare arms. I snatched away from her quickly.

"What the hell? Are you crazy." I stared at her rubbing my smarting arm. This woman had been giving me the cold shoulder and the stank eye since we'd met. Her putting her hands on me was crossing a serious line. Instead of smacking this bitch, I took the high road and continued towards the bathroom, giving her a warning glare as I did. But her words stopped me in my tracks.

"You American Bitch," she hissed just loud enough so only I could hear her.

I chuckled as I tossed my braids over my shoulder, "Like mother like daughter. Funny how Mackena parroted the same thing to me

the first night I met you both." I sucked my teeth at her, continuing my stride to the restroom.

She didn't relent. "I should have made him and that stupid
whore of a mother abort you." This time it was her who chuckled out loud. I turned back to see her studying her nails as if she
were already too bored with the conversation.

Looking up, she continued as if the thought had just occurred to her. "Oh. You didn't know?" Kwam offered a pitying
smile at my confused stare.

"Well dear, your mother wanted to abort you when she
couldn't have him. She knew about me from the beginning.
And orchestrated getting pregnant to tie your father down."

I said nothing, gutted by what Kwam said next.

"When the fool realized it wouldn't work she tried to abort
you. Oh yes, made the appointment and everything. Was all but
on the table, machines about to slurp you out or her vile pussy.
Had it not been for your Aunt Vi, letting Leboo know. You'd
be pulp, my dear. Without him, you were just an unwanted
pregnancy." She laughed bitterly at the stricken look on my
face.

"And the simpleton of a man your father was, he convinced her
that he was in love with her and kept her from doing it. All these
years you thought he abandoned you. No dear, your mother didn't
want you. And he couldn't have her. Or you for that matter. His

oh so precious first born," her face was now a scowl as if the taste
of me being his precious first born would make her wretch.

Kwam kept going. "And here you are parading across the stage
like you're somebody. You are the unwanted, uncultured, illegiti-
mate, brat of a whor—"

Before she let the word whore in regard to my mother slip
between her lips one more time, I reached to the pit of my soul
and slapped her ass into that fountain. I immediately regretted it
because instantaneously flashes from several cameras started going
off.

Chapter 23 —Kobe

♥

ONE MOMENT, I WAS standing there talking about the lack of diversity in chefs of Michelin-starred restaurants and the "French" bias in the rating system. The next moment, all hell broke loose.

An armed security guard walked up, grabbing my arm and pulled me in the direction Andra had gone off to the restroom. Speaking into an earpiece, he said, "I found him sir. We're on the way to you."

Moving as fast as he was pulling me, I asked, "What's going on? Where's Andra?"

"This way, Sir." He continued pulling me through throngs of people. The scene before me was chaos as we entered the hotel through the back door from the gardens.

Andra's father was helping a very wet, very angry woman out of the fountain. I surmised that she was his wife, the wicked stepmother Andra had only briefly told me about.

The head of security, Okiyo, whom I'd met when I was picked up from the airport, was barking orders for members of the press to step back. Upon seeing me, he nodded in Andra's direction then yelled, "Get her out of here. SUV is waiting outside."

My feet moved of their own volition towards Andra. I was momentarily blinded from the flash of a camera that was surreptitiously stuck in my face. I took her hand and led her away from the party, not caring about the cameras or the paparazzi. All I cared about was her and making sure she was okay.

As we were driving back to Andra's condo, she was silent but I could see the pain etched on her face and the tears that threatened to spill over and they did the moment we made it into her condo. She crumbled. I caught her as we slid to the floor together and I held her close.

She trembled, shoulders quaking as she cried; her breaths coming in short gasps. It was clear that whatever happened between her and her stepmother had shaken her to the core. And as we sat there, her agony was palpable.

When her sobbing subsided, I stroked her braids. "Andra," I whispered, "What happened, baby girl?"

"I ran into Kwam," she said, her voice trembling. "And she said some really fucked up shit about my mom."

My heart sank. I knew that Kwam was Andra's stepmother, but I had never met her before. Andra had told me she was a piece of work, but I thought it ended at her not wanting her husband's love child around. I guess it would stand to reason that she'd have some shit to say about the love child's mama too.

"What did she say?" I asked, trying to keep my voice calm.

Andra looked up at me, tears streaming down her face. "That I should have been aborted. Was nearly aborted."

"What?" I said, stunned.

She fidgeted with the beaded bracelet on her wrist, then looked at me with pure pain etched into every line of her face. "She said that my mother got pregnant with me in an effort to trap my father and force him to marry her. And when it didn't work, she tried to abort me. Had it not been for my father getting to the abortion clinic just in time, I would have been terminated."

My blood boiled. How could someone say something like this? True or not, Andra had nothing to do with their sordid circle jerk back in the day. I pulled her in tighter. She buried her head in my chest still trembling from her sobs.

"That's when I lost it," Andra continued after a while. At first her voice was muffled by my shirt but got stronger as she pulled away, tears replaced by her fire. "I tried to slap that Bitch's teeth down her throat. She better be glad that fountain caught her ass." I couldn't help the quick chuckle that slipped. A smile tickled at the corners of my mouth. This was the Andra I knew.

I pulled her back in tightly, glad to see her spunk, still feeling a mix of anger and sadness at Kwam's words. Regardless of their validity, they were meant to hurt and maim Andra. And they did.

"It's okay," I whispered, stroking her hair. "Fuck Kwam. She's bitter and hurt. Evelyn loves you." But even as I said the words, I could feel Andra's hurt surrounding her mother's attempted abortion building again.

"All these years, I thought my daddy didn't want me, but it was her. I've always been some kind of mistake."

"Kwam just said those things to hurt you, Andra." I implored, turning her to face me. It was clear my words landed on deaf ears.

"Kobe, you don't understand," Andra said, pulling away from me. "There's something that my aunt Vivian said to my mother before I came to Kenya."

And as Andra spoke, I could see the determination in her eyes, the steel in her voice.

"She said that my mother had pulled some kind of stunt with my father, and that it had backfired. That she had been a cold bitch ever since. And now... I can't help but believe there's some truth to all this."

I didn't know what to say. Her voice shook with raw emotion as she continued. "Kobe, I feel so alone. An unwanted mista—"

"Andra," I said, shaking her, "You're nobody's gawd-damned mistake!" I cupped her face gently in my hands and looked into her eyes reassuringly, "I'm here for you. I've always been here."

That was when she leaned in towards me and softly pressed her lips to mine—tentatively at first but gradually deepening, searching, questioning. I knew I should've stopped her. She was emotional. Grasping for her lifeline. But I couldn't. She was my lifeline too. I loved this girl with all that was me. Despite our bond of platonic friendship. Despite Carmel and what I'd been fooling myself into believing could be something real. I loved Andra fiercely and I crushed her to me, praying that she'd come to the same conclusion.

When her tongue snaked between my lips, I knew that what we shared was deeper than just friendship; that kiss was a connection that was both physical and spiritual. The air around us sizzled, carrying a current of unspoken understanding—as if nothing else mattered.

She pulled away, a wisp of a smile showing on her tear-streaked face. I barely heard her when she said it first. "I love you, Kobe."

"I love you too, Andra," I said, pulling her in for another more passionate and raw kiss. Our mouths parted and we explored each other further with caresses, stroking each other's skin with a newfound intimacy. Time seemed to stand still as our bodies intertwined together while we explored one another under the moonlight that shone through the wall of windows.

She'd already tugged the sleeves of my tux down and off as we fought to be closer to each other. She now faced away swinging her long braids over her shoulder to expose the zipper of her dress. I pulled it down releasing the dress to fall in a satin blue heap at her feet. She reached back to unfasten the bra and turned. The air was sucked out of the room at the sight of her. She was beautiful.

I closed my eyes, breathing in sharply before quickly closing the space between us. Her hands were pressed tight between our bodies as she unfastened the tiny buttons of my shirt and pushed it over my shoulders.

Our eyes caught. Mine exploring the depths of hers, looking for any sign that she wanted me to stop. I saw none as her hands glided over my chest as if to memorize its peaks and valleys. I caught one of her wrists in my hands bringing her fingers up to kiss each one of them. I moaned when her other hand wandered lower, grazing my taught erection through the front of my trousers.

She had unfastened the hook and bar and released the zipper of my pants. My knees buckled slightly at the sensation of her warm hand slipping beneath the band of my briefs, gripping firmly around the length of my erection. I almost called her name when her thumb pressed against the seeping eye of my head and slipped concentric circles in the precum. My nerve endings synapsed shooting pleasure through my groin.

I bent to lick the tip of one of her exposed nipples. Squeezing the dime sized stiff buds between my thumb and forefinger, before sucking as much of it and her breast greedily between my lips. She moaned as she threw her head back in pleasure, her hand gently stroking my dick. I lifted from one nipple ready to assault the other when my damn cell began to ring.

It was in the breast pocket of my tuxedo jacket that was on the arm of the couch. I ignored it, letting it roll to voicemail, as I sought out Andra's mouth. Our tongues slipped and intertwined with each other before I captured hers, sucking it into my mouth as mine swiped and darted in hers, exploring the depths when my phone rang again.

The spell was broken as she pulled away, pulling my face down to rest my forehead against hers as she whispered breathily, "You better get that."

I took a steadying breath as well, jerking the phone from my pocket. I squinted at the screen before quickly moving to answer it.

"Dad. What's wrong?" I asked when I heard the trouble in his voice. "Fuck! Is she ok?" I yelled. "I'm on the way."

I hung up the phone, turning to Andra. "There was another break in at the restaurant –"

"Another?" Andra questioned frantically.

"I'll explain later. My mom was there when they broke in this time and was hurt. I have to get to the airport."

"I'm coming with you!" she said, pushing past me to her room to grab a bag.

Chapter 24 – Andra

♥

OUR FLIGHT LANDED IN Atlanta at around 3PM. Kobe damn near drug me through the airport to the Uber lane outside where our car was already waiting. Winded, we jumped into the backseat as I shakily pressed the sequence of numbers to call my father to let him know we'd made it. While Kobe implored the driver to hurry to the hospital

"Andra," my father hesitated, measuring his words. "Have you seen the news?"

"No, we literally ran off the plane to the waiting Uber Kobe ordered." I'd literally just turned my phone on minutes before and dialed his number before it could boot up good. And just like that, both my phone and Kobe's began going berserk with notifications. Mine in my ear, Kobe's in his hand.

"Umm... Hold on a second," I said, pulling my phone away from my ear to open the notifications window. The first notification in a list of about 20 and growing, read "Atlanta Food blogger/Socialite

Just Outed as Secret Child of African Billionaire... Mmm and that ain't all" above a picture of me slapping Kwam. That was TMZ.

The Shade Room had posted, "Atlanta Native and Well-known Social Media Influencer, Andra Bainswright, Reported to Have Scammed Her Way to the Top of the Social Media Ladder."

"It Girl, Rich Girl, or Fraud? Half of the Duo @Gastrafrique has Some Explaining to Do!" ... and they kept rolling in, getting uglier and uglier with each ding.

"Andra! Are you there?" I heard my dad yelling through my haze of shock.

"Y- Yeah. Yes. I'm here," I stammered, groaning at the implications of these nasty reports coming out just before the airing of the show. "None of this scamming stuff is true." I said after the initial shock wore off.

"Don't worry! You and Kobe get to the hospital. Okiyo and I are on the way. We'll need to straighten this out with the studio. In the meantime, Andra, stay out of the public eye!"

I let the phone dangle in my lap as I fought the urge to totally fall apart. I couldn't. The negative posts were about me. All lies, except for me slapping Kwam. I found myself more angry that not one of those articles even mentioned the break-in at Gastrafrique and an innocent bystander getting injured in the process.

Kobe had been reading through the alerts just as I had. He reached across the seat and grabbed my hand. "I told 'ya all that

scamming would catch up to ya *gyul*." He said, smiling and winking at me. Just like him trying to make me feel better even in spite
of dealing with his own pain. His mother had been attacked and
was in the hospital.

He pecked my lips before his face grew serious again. "Your dad
is right. We need to stay out of the spotlight." He leaned forward
and tapped the Uber driver on the shoulder, "Can you make a stop
to drop her off before we get to the hosp—"

"Oh hell no, Kobe," I said vehemently, shaking my head, "There
is nothing that's going to stop me from going to that hospital with
you!"

"But Andra, the show –"

"Fuck that show! Somebody broke into our restaurant and hurt
your mom. I need to make sure she is ok." I glared at him. "Sir
please continue to the hospital." The Uber driver's eyes shifted
from Kobe's to mine and back to Kobe's not sure what to do until
Kobe nodded his head in acquiescence to my demand.

When we pulled up to the emergency room entrance, media vans
and news reporters were everywhere. We had to fight through the
throng of them to get to the door. Thank God, security had barred
them from entering. Kobe and I both nodded our thanks and ran

to the information station to find out where his mother's room was. We took off down the hall, hand in hand, Kobe leading the way.

I could hear Mr. Abara fussing over his wife even before we got through the room door.

"Let the woman do her job, Belle!"

"Oh hush. I told y'all I'm fine. Just a little knot."

"Woman, you have a concussion so be still and let the lady check you out."

The lady in question was the nurse and she was giggling at the banter between the Abara's as she made her rounds, checking the IV and the bandage around Ms. Abara's head.

"Sounds like we rushed here for nothing," Kobe said, as soon as we entered the room.

"Kobe," Mr. Abara jumped up from his seat to come around his wife's bed to greet his son.

"Now I know damn well you didn't jump on a plane to rush back here to see about me," Mrs. Abara said, sucking her teeth at her son, knowing full well she was glad to see him.

Due to the setup of the entryway into the room and the broadness of Kobe's body, neither of his parents had seen me yet. The surprise on their faces, especially Mrs. Abara's when I stepped around Kobe and answered for the both of us, "Yes, we did, Ma'am!" Was priceless, as I sucked my teeth right back at her, unable to hold the stern look on my face as I mimicked the one she was giving Kobe.

"Andra? Oh ,Andra, you're here too," Mrs. Abara said excitedly, face splitting into a huge smile when she realized I was there. She smiled even harder when she looked down and saw mine and Kobe's hands still intertwined. She didn't say anything, but the sly grin she gave when I tried to quickly let his hand go and he held on tighter, told her what we'd be doing later. Mrs. Abara gushed, "*Gyul*, get over We miss ya so!"

He was amused at the consternation on my face at us getting caught holding hands. I shot him a daggered glance, before rushing to the bed to throw my arms around his mother.

The nurse who'd been in the room making her rounds, cleared her throat, thankfully getting everyone's attention before she left the room. "Alright now. Looks like y'all have some catching up to do. But Mrs. Abara, do take it easy!"

I quickly pulled back at the nurse's words, making sure I wasn't hurting her, I straightened from the bed, keeping some distance between me and Kobe. He was more than happy to blast our recent turn of feelings from the rooftop. I wasn't quite ready to explain just yet.

He turned to the nurse and asked, "How is she?" Knowing full well his mom would give him the watered-down version of the truth.

Looking back and forth between Kobe and I the nurse responded, "She's fine, but we are still running a few tests to make sure there's no internal swelling in her head. She took a hard blow, but that one there," she paused looking over at Mrs. Abara, "is a hellion. Didn't go down without a fight. Even managed to scratch up one of the assailants, too. Detectives came by yesterday and already collected DNA samples." She smiled, shaking her head, amused appreciation for Mrs. Abara's tenacity, as she exited the room.

Kobe sat on the edge of the hospital bed to further inspect his mom to make sure she was ok, while I sat by Mr. Abara and joked around with him as we normally did, telling him all about my trip to Kenya, filming the tv show, and the Maasai Mara. I left out the parts about meeting my dad and the drama with Kwam... They'd find out about that soon enough.

Mrs. Abara caught my attention when she was retelling to Kobe what happened during the break-in.

"I went in to meet with the photographer, just like you asked me to. He got some great photos of the food by the way," she waved a hand in the air. "Everything went off without a hitch. It was dark after they left so I was going to the back to shut off the lights and everything and as soon as I stepped into the back office, the door came crashing in. I hadn't set the alarm yet, but they seemed shocked that I was still in the building. It was two of them. I ran around the desk to grab the phone and dial 911 but didn't get all the numbers in before one of them, Keelan, or something like that hit me."

"Wait. Did you say, Keland?" I asked Mrs. Abara, shifting my eyes to meet Kobe's.

"Yes. Keland!" She snapped her finger at the name. "When the other guy grabbed me to keep me from dialing 911, we fought over the phone until I scratched his face. I stunned him pretty good and he yelled, 'this bitch cut me, Keland!' Next thing you know the room went black.

Chapter 25 –Kobe

♥

WHILE WE WERE IN the hospital room, Andra's dad called from the airport. He and Okiyo were about to board his private jet on their way here. He assured both Andra and I that everything would be alright and that Okiyo had put some of his men on finding out who had broken into the restaurant. He had a hunch that it was the same person or group who was leaking the nasty rumors about Andra to the media.

Leboo speculated and I agreed that it wasn't a coincidence that the break-in at the restaurant and the altercation between Andra and Kwam, two events that happened on opposite sides of the world, would break at the same time in the media. That paired with the allegations of Andra being a scammer, spoke to insider threat. Someone close enough to me or Andra was responsible for this.

Because of this, he'd asked that both Andra and I lay low until he and his people could figure this all out. He'd used his connections to hire us a car and had already booked two rooms for us at the Hyatt Regency downtown to keep the media off our tails.

We'd settled into our adjoining rooms and jet lag was creeping in but my mom's account of the break-in at the restaurant paired with Leboo's suspicions wouldn't let me rest.

I prepared to knock on the adjoining door to our rooms, but it was snatched open before I could. Andra walked in, arms folded tight across her chest, face drawn. Obviously unsettled. She sat at the foot of my bed, drawn look on her face.

She didn't say anything, so I did. "You don't think that simp as nigga you was fucking with before going to Africa is behind this, do you?"

She lowered her forehead to her palms, blowing out a sigh. She slowly wiped her open hands down the length of her face, before looking at me. Obviously asking herself the same question.

Apologetically, she whispered, "Can't say it wasn't the first thing that crossed my mind, Kobe." Her shoulders sank forcing her head to drop back, eyes lifted to the ceiling as if the answer to my question was written there. Her eyes found mine, beseeching. "I mean, we only went on a couple of dates. Why would he do that?"

"Yeah, but *baby'gyul*, didn't you ghost him?" I asked cautiously, sliding onto the bed to sit beside her. I didn't want her to think I was blaming her for the break-in. But I also had to fight the urge to grill her about her interactions with another man. Regardless of my feelings for her, it wasn't my place. I had all but stood by idly for years, watching her do her thing. Admittedly, it was hard to watch. But I did, instead of letting her know how I felt about her.

Her head dropped; eyes cast down before she finally spoke. "I wouldn't quite consider it ghosting. Not immediately anyway."

"What would you consider it to be then, Andra? You even said yourself that 'this one might be a keeper' when y'all went out on that last date. You do remember that don't you?"

"Of course I remember," she said, eyes darting quickly away.

"What are you not saying?" I asked, knowing when she was leaving out some important detail. "Did you sleep with him again? If it is him spreading these vicious rumors, there's got to be more to the story than just a couple of dates and a one-night stand, Andra. Did something else happen between the two of you?"

This time Andra moved away creating space, her eyes trained on the patterns in the carpet. She steepled her fingers under her lips before quietly saying, "I slept with him again. Just before leaving to go to Kenya," squeezing her eyes shut before continuing, "He told me he wanted to be exclusive. Then everything happened at once with the tv show and the restaurant deals and I, uhhh," she hesitated then shifted her eyes to me. "I back-burnered him."

Her eyes were pleading for my understanding. She looked small sitting beside me, shoulders drooped. Embarrassed. Apologetic and scared.

Fucking and fleeing had been her coping mechanism. I knew this. I'd watched her do it a million times before but didn't judge. It's how she fought the demons born of deep daddy issues. I loved her enough to look away. At some point even took responsibility for healing her hurt.

I moved closer, closing the space she'd created between us. I cupped her chin and tilted her face up to mine. "Baby 'gyul, I'm not judging, just trying to see if this motherfucker has a motive." I kissed her forehead and pulled her into my chest as her body vibrated from her silent sobs.

After a while, her small voice spoke, "He called a few times before I left to go to Kenya... I was all over the place trying to wrap my head around the tv show, being away from you, getting things in order, so I just let him go to voicemail. Thinking he'd get the point."

"Well what did the messages say?"

She looked down at the iPhone in her lap before groaning. "I don't know. He left them on my Android. I didn't have service on it in Kenya," she said now holding the iPhone up with a lopsided grimace. "Wait a minute. My other phone might be in my carryon bag." She jumped from the bed quickly covering the distance between the rooms. A few minutes later, she came back empty handed. "I guess I left it back at the condo in Nairobi."

She walked back over to the bed, exhaustion all over her. I pulled her down into my lap and she turned in my arms placing her cheek on my chest. "Kobe, we need to talk about last night."

"What's there to talk about? I told you on the plane that I love you. Have for a long time. Just didn't want to make things awkward." I looked down at her and chuckled. "Plus, you never gave a brother a chance."

"I love you too Kobe. That's not it though. I only realized it was more than just 'I love you as my friend or my homeboy,' while I was in Kenya. And it did get awkward," she said as she tilted her head back, eyes closed.

Blowing out a deep breath. She leveled her eyes on mine before continuing. "I just don't want us to fuck up our friendship." She clasped my hand, pulling it to her chest. "Once the line is crossed, we can't go back. We'll never be the same."

"It will only be awkward if we make it awkward," I paused to plant a kiss on her forehead. But pulled back and looked at her when I thought about her admission of only discovering her feelings for me had changed while she was in Kenya. "Andra, what happened that made you realize your feelings had changed."

Her face balled as she moaned, "I knew you were going to ask me that..." After a brief chuckle, she scrunched her face and blurted, "I saw you naked in your kitchen." She looked at me, face still scrunched, eyebrows raised to see my reaction.

"What?" I laughed too, pulling her hands away from her face. "What do you mean you saw me naked in my kitchen? Girl what are you talking about?"

"It was the first day we rode our Pelotons together when I first got there.—"

"Well we only worked out one time. You ghosted me every other time we were supposed to work out together."

"Yeah, about that." she muttered, obviously stalling.

"Spit it out, woman. How did you see me naked?"

"You forgot to turn off the camera on your bike," she blurted, "When I got back on mine I had clear sight into your kitchen and while I was trying to turn my camera off, you walked into the kitchen, and..." Her voice trailed off again, This time her face brightened as if savoring the memory.

"Oh. Ohhh," I said, remembering that day clearly. We both were silent for a few minutes. Then a thought occurred. "Is that why you were ducking my calls?"

Again, she looked away. "It's part of the reason."

"Well what's the other part?"

"I dreamed about it. I mean you. *Fuck.*" She pulled in and blew out a sharp breath. "I had a dream about us. In the kitchen at Jah, your old restaurant. We were under the big spice rack on that back wall."

It took a moment for what she was saying to sink in. When it finally did, I burst out laughing as she sat there staring at me in disbelief.

"I tell you that I saw your big ass dick and had a dream that you were about to use that monster on me and all you can do is laugh?" She said scowling at me.

"Andra, if I had a dollar for every wet dream I've had about you over the years, I'd me a millionaire. Tell me one thing though?"

"What?" she said, looking at me through narrowed eyes.

"Was it good?"

Stunned, she reached back her hand to pop me upside my head like she'd done so many times over the years when I said something to shock her. Anticipating her move, I grabbed her cocked hand, pulling it to my lips again, kissing each of her fingertips before placing her palm over my heart. "I've waited a lifetime to say I love you, and to hear you say it back. That's all I needed to hear from you."

She looked at me with pure love in her eyes. When she spoke, it came out in a whisper. "We never finished."

"What do you mean?" I asked.

"You asked me if it was good?" She pulled me down beside her on the bed. "Both times I've had a chance to explore you, in my dream... last night, we never had a chance to finish."

I kissed her as realization dawned. "How about we find out now?"

She looked at me with a question on her lips, when I moved to kneel in front of her at the foot of the bed and reached beneath the hem of the sleep shirt she'd changed into when we got to the room. I was pleasantly surprised to find she wasn't wearing any panties.

I kept my eyes on her when I gripped the meaty flesh of her hips and pulled her essence to meet my face at the edge of the bed.

Her eyes glazed, the moment my warm breath met the apex of her thighs. She whimpered when the wet warmth of my tongue met the wet slickness of her lower lips. She gripped my head between her hands when my tongue breached her lips and made a long swipe up and over her already swollen clit. She tasted delicious. She moaned and her head fell back when I pulled her closer and suckled her clit, swiping my tongue over the sensitive ligaments on top of her hooded pearl.

Her body convulsed as a slipped first one, then two fingers inside her, still swirling my tongue around her clit. Her juices coated my entire hand as I pumped my fingers in and out of her and her pussy gripped and spasmed around them tightly.

Andra panted, barely able to say my name as I continued to finger fuck her into a frenzy. When she cried out, "Kobe," followed by a long moan that ripped from her lips, I quickly removed my fingers then dipped my head, firming my tongue before dipping it into the sweet, puckered opening of her ass.

She spasmed again, a cry of absolute pleasure wrenched from her lips. She was close to cumming. and I wanted to give her a finish. I swiped my tongue back up past the puckered star I'd just assaulted, swirling my tongue around her sphincter, then up across her perineum, dipping it into her wet pussy. I finally landed back on her convulsing clit. Sucking and reinserting two fingers into her pussy. I pumped and sucked until she exploded in an orgasm that lifted her back off the bed.

When the tremors in her body subsided and her breathing eased, I layed beside her and cradled her to my chest until we both fell asleep.

We sat in the living room on Andra's side of our adjoining suite in abject shock. Leboo sat across from us alone as he laid out what Okiyo was able to dig up while they were enroute to At-lanta. It was a considerable amount to take in. His suspicions of the rumors slandering Andra and Gastrafrique were confirmed.

"Keland," we said in unison before her dad could say the name. He nodded his head in agreement.

"Okiyo is already in contact with the detectives on the case. He admittedly thought you were behind the break-ins, Kobe. You being in Kenya when this one happened has exonerated you fully."

"Yeah. That motherfu—sorry. Same detective that questioned me after the first break in. He made it abundantly clear that he thought I may have had something to do with it. Guess he thought I was trying to get an insurance pay out or something."

"No need to apologize, son. I understand your frustration."

Andra's father shook his head, pressing his lips together in a thin-lipped smile. "It would seem that not much has changed with the American legal system since I was here all those years ago. Black men in this country are still viewed as guilty until proven innocent."

Getting back to business, Leboo clapped his hands, steepling them under a narrow-eyed stare as if going over a mental checklist. "Now, Okiyo will handle Keland and law enforcement," he said, "He'll get to the bottom of this break-in nonsense. Andra," he directed his attention at her, "We are going to have to smooth all this over with the networks. Considering the scamming allegations, they are skeptical about launching the show until all this blows over."

Andra was crestfallen. Leboo assured her that once he flew out to L.A. in the next day or so to talk with the studio, level heads would surely prevail.

He continued, "By now, I'm sure they've all watched the footage and know they have a money-making hit on their hands. This will all be over soon my dear. Especially since it looks like Keland may be behind spreading the rumors as well.

"He certainly has the motive," I co-signed his statement.

With that Leboo sat back in his seat but leveled his gaze back on Andra. "My dear, I am sorry I wasn't around to teach you the fragility of men. Some can't handle rejection from the opposite sex once they've latched on. Let this be a lesson to you," he chided brows raised above a knowing look. "But on second thought, I don't think that'll be a problem in the future if this vibe I'm reading off the two of you is correct."

You could have heard a rat piss on cotton. It got so quiet in the room. Andra's jaw dropped and I had to unglue my eyes off of Leboo's grinning face after the initial shock of his words wore off. Not wanting to hide my feelings any longer, I grabbed Andra's hand and smiled at her as she sat there, eyes wide as if caught with her hand in the cookie jar.

Leboo, threw his head back and laughed heartily. For a second breaking his buttoned up, polished demeanor. "Oh don't look so shocked. You two have an electrifying chemistry. I saw it the first time that I logged into a Gastrafrique live on IG. You'd have to be virtually blind, dumb and deaf to not see the love in this man's eyes when he looks at you.

"Consider me blind, dumb and deaf then." Andra said, finally breaking her silence.

Finally sobering, Leboo once again trained his eyes on Andra. There is one more thing that I think we need to fix while I'm here. He looked at his daughter. "Would you mind indulging your father and riding with me on a..." he paused, thoughtfully, "Personal errand?"

Chapter 26 – Andra

♥

I KNEW SHE WOULDN'T be home so I gave my dad's driver the address to the gallery. It was just past 8PM on a Monday, near closing time. I knew that all clients and customers would be gone by now and she'd be in the back storeroom cataloging the art that had either newly arrived or was ready to go on display.

Hearing the door chime, my mother came out of the back storeroom. Pausing to smooth her dress down and walk towards the front before greeting the potential patron. I could see her, but she couldn't see me yet.

I walked the long way around the high walls to prolong the surprise. She didn't yet know, I was back. She certainly wasn't aware that I would have company. *Not this company, for damn sure.*

She was patting her hair to ensure not a strand was out of place as she started quickly walking to the front of the studio. She paused suddenly, tilting her ear at the sound of my pointed heels on the hardwood floor. First, her face scrunched, then a broad smile broke across her face in recognition of my gate. "Andra?"

Two steps later I was in plain view. She jumped with glee at the sight of me. *Evelyn, gleeful? She must have really missed me.* She did a quick trot towards me in her own sky-high stilettos throwing her arms open for a hug. "Girl, I know that long, heavy walk anywhere."

"It's me," I squealed, closing the gap between us to embrace her in the hug. It was so good to be in her arms, I totally forgave her "heavy walk" comment. This was my mom. Hell I'd gotten my quick tongue honestly.

"I wasn't expecting you back from Kenya so soon." She exclaimed, eyes flitting away briefly at the mere mention of the word Kenya. When she trained her eyes back on me, her unguarded expression, pleasant though it was, settled on me with a look somewhere between motherly concern and aloof professionalism.

"What is all this mess I'm hearing about you on the news, child?" She asked, placing a hand on her hip, then dropping it quickly to reach for my hand. "Nevermind all that, you're home. I missed you so—" Her words trailed off and her face went rigid as she stared past me.

"Oh, um... I should have told you that I brought a visitor with me," I smiled wryly, cringing internally as I looked back and forth between my mother's frozen glare and my father's boyish gaze. She may as well have seen a ghost as her eyes locked on the eyes of her long-lost lover. While he was looking like he'd found his long-lost angel.

They were locked into memories of their past as I looked on, watching a million emotions flit across both of their faces. And if what I saw between the two of them was anything akin to the chemistry that my father said blanketed Kobe and I, I think I might have witnessed what true love really was; in living color.

I knew then what my mother had lost so many years ago. For the first time, I saw her as a woman. A woman with a past that was more than just being my mom. And I understood. Understood her heartache. Her *heartbreak*.

Through the look she gave him, I saw justification why she'd hardened her heart and threw herself into work. As a child, I couldn't understand. As a woman I knew she did the best she could despite me being the living reminder of the love she lost.

At that moment, I didn't need answers about any of the vile things Kwam had said. Hell, I understood her pain too. Knowing that the man you were forced to marry would never love you the way he loved, and from the looks of it still loves, another woman.

I cleared my throat and squeezed my mother's hand. Her composure faltered and she swatted a tear that escaped down her cheek. I gave her an encouraging smile before announcing, "Mom. Dad. I think you two may know each other."

They both laughed tentatively, as I smiled on. They really looked like two skittish high school kids who didn't know what to say to each other. I was just glad the ice was broken a little as they warmed up.

I told my mom all about my trip to Kenya, glazing over the circumstances of how I discovered who my father was. I told her about the show and filming on the Maasai Mara. All the while, I could see them stealing glances at each other. Before long, they began to actually talk.

Both shared stories about me as a child before he left. We all laughed as my dad told a story that I absolutely didn't remember about me taking his expensive Cuban cigars that he loved out to the back yard and using them to stir the mud I'd been mixing to make mud pies. My mother laughed so hard, retelling how my dad moped around for a week about those cigars. My heart was full. This was a moment I never thought I'd witness. My family, however brief, was together again.

These two needed to catch up way more than my mom and I did. I looked at my watch and looked towards my father, faking a yawn.

"Whew, this jet lag is still kicking my butt. Why don't you two finish catching up. Go grab some drinks or something." All the while edging toward the door. "I'm going to have the driver drop me off at the hotel. You kids have fun."

I rushed out the door, a huge grin on my face before either could stop me.

I was preparing to use the keycard to enter my room when I noticed Kobe's light still on under his room door. Good he's still awake. I couldn't wait to tell him about the events that just unfolded between my mom and dad. I knocked and stood back waiting for him to open.

Minutes went by. No answer. But I could hear him shuffling around so I knew he was there. I knocked again. Louder this time. Before I made the third strike, the door wrenched open revealing a wet, bare-chested Kobe. He stood there wrapped only in a towel clearly fresh out of the shower. A flashback from our post video Peloton workout played fresh in my mind.

I found myself standing there, transfixed by the sight of his chiseled chest, unable to tear my gaze away from the rock-solid peaks before me. I had to physically inhale air and close my eyes to pull my thoughts away from what the towel was hiding. It was knotted right above his...thick... knot. And I knew exactly what that knot looked like. And wanted to savor every inch of Kobe's monster.

When my eyes finally slid up to meet his, he was watching me with amusement. Eyes as glazed with lust as mine, and a daring smirk playing at the corners of his mouth. I knew the look well. The one he'd given me several times over the years daring me to do something... daring. But this time, he was the dare.

He moved almost imperceptibly, making way to let me in the door. I moved to walk past him into his room. He circled my waist with his thick corded arms, pulling me into him. And here we were— His chest to my back, hard dick poking me through that towel.

It was funny how my childhood best friend had me blushing and shy like a schoolgirl, when all these years, I'd been the aggressor in all things, including with the men I'd dated and discarded over the years. Now, Kobe had me biting my lips and praying that he'd kiss me. I spun around facing him and studied his features. He was caught up in a rapture that I was the center of and took his time.

First he placed a soft kiss on my forehead. Next, each eyelid. Slow and beautiful. By the time he made a trail of kisses to my neck, he was growing harder under the towel draped around his waist. The sensation of his growing thickness pressing into my belly melted me. All thoughts of telling him about how the reunion between my mom and dad went evaporated.

The sensation was too much. Visions of the dream I'd had of us in the kitchen at Jah invaded my senses. His tongue dancing in the soft spot at the base of my neck just above my beating pulse point, had my pussy throbbing to a smooth Afrobeats rhythm of Kobe's creation.

His hands traversed slowly up my arms, meeting the straps of the silk shift dress I wore sliding them down. The dress slid down my body, pooling at our feet. Never lifting his lips from my neck, he unclasped the black strapless bra freeing my breasts.

When my pebbled nipples grazed the solid warmth of his chest, I melted. I was lava the moment he shifted his mouth up to mine. I was consumed when he whispered, "We've wasted enough time. Come to me."

His lips crashed into mine. He kissed me so deeply. His tongue swiped against mine hungrily. He explored the recesses of my mouth. I couldn't breathe and I couldn't care less. Couldn't be close enough to him. I ripped at the towel, now the only thing between us and I died and went to heaven when the full heavy length of him molded between our bodies.

Kobe scooped me up, kicked the towel out of the way and carried me to the wall of glass at the far side of the room. The soft light from the still ajar bathroom was the only light, which made the 24th floor view of Atlanta all the more spectacular at night.

He slowly lowered my feet to the floor and turned me around to look out at the view as he wrapped his arms around me pulling my back to meet his chest. He bent to whisper, "You remember telling me all those years ago that when you finally made it big, you were going to celebrate by getting fucked on the top floor of the Westin downtown?"

I turned to look up at him in surprise. "You remember that?" I whispered.

"Yes," He said softly, resting his chin on the top of my head. "I remember everything about you. It was the first time I wanted to be the one, the only one who fucked you."

My sharp intake of breath made him chuckle ever so softly as he turned me around to face him.

"Well this ain't the Westin baby and I don't want to fuck you. But I do want to make love to the only woman I've ever loved on the 24th floor of the Hyatt Regency overlooking the city tonight." He looked me deep in the eye and asked, "Andra, can I make love to you tonight and every night for the rest of our lives?"

"You better, Kobena Abara."

And then he picked me up, wrapping my legs around his waist and pushing my back into the cold glass. His dick sank into me, slowly and I opened completely to this man, like I'd never opened to any other. Every stroke was a building wave threatening to wash over us. And I wanted to drown. Drown him completely in my ocean.

I held on for dear life and let my best friend, my protector and now my lover imprint his name on my soul and I cried. Tears of pure release in the safety of this man.

He carried me to the bed after I exploded, coming all over his dick. The dick I'd been curious about, dreamed about, stayed buried deep inside me as he laid me on the bed and proceeded to make love to me until he pulled out and came in thick creamy rivulets between our bellies.

We lay there in silence for a moment, him still holding me tight. I lay partially under him, one leg wrapped around one of his possessively, reflecting back on our love making. The way I felt about this man right now, he could have shot the club all the way up and I would have gladly walked around anxiously for weeks wondering if I was having his baby. The thought made me giggle.

Kobe stirred, to ask, "A penny for your thoughts?"

"Mmm," I moaned, lifting my head up to plant a soft kiss on his lips. "I'm just amazed at how much of a mess you just made on these folks' sheets."

"That made you laugh?" he asked, chuckling softly himself knowing that his nut wasn't all that I'd been thinking about.

"Well if you must know. I was thinking that we didn't use a condom."

"Okay," he said, expecting more.

"And... *Baybayyy* the way you put it down on me, I wouldn't have cared if you skeed all up in these walls!" I finished. Now his turn to chuckle.

"Is that right?" he asked, cupping a hand on my ass, and pulling me into his side. "A little Andra running around ain't such a bad idea," he said soberly, this time gently cupping my chin, pulling my face to his. "You would make a great mother, Andra."

"I've never really thought about it before. Children that is. Never wanted a situation like mine and my moms, you know."

"Your mom did the best she could, I'm sure."

"Yeah. I know. Speaking of which," I shifted to lay on Kobe's chest. "You should have seen the look on her face when my dad walked into the gallery. Kobe, she tried to play it cool, but the look she gave that man... She was like a schoolgirl. Red and flushed as ever. I've never seen Evelyn Bainswright flustered. The chemistry between the two of them was undeniable and he was just as taken away as she was."

"Wow. They say true love never dies. Did they get a chance to clear the air?"

"Well," I said thoughtfully before continuing, "I left them at the gallery."

"Whoa, your mother hates him, doesn't she?"

"Uh, yeah. So I thought. It was supposed to be just a quick pop in so my Dad could open the door for reconciliation, but what I witnessed between the two of them, I had to get out of the way so they could see it through, my boy. No hate was detected at all on Evelyn Bainswright, Sir." I said, snapping my finger to punctuate the unexpected turn in events.

We lay there for a while longer, wrapped in each other's familiarity. Before long, Kobe's monster began to stir. He nuzzled my neck with his nose, until I shifted my weight allowing him to hover above me. He plunged deep and just laid in my depths for a moment savoring my warmth.

I opened for him yet again, ready to receive him over and over throughout the night. I had a feeling we were about to try to catch up for all the time we'd lost.

Chapter 27 –Kobe

♥

FOR THE BETTER PART of the week since we'd gotten back from Kenya, the media had been on Andra's and my every move. At the behest of Andra's father, we'd pretty much been holed up in our hotel rooms to let the storm blow over. Of course this wasn't a bad problem to have since the majority of the time was spent with me and Andra exploring each other's bodies. On every flat surface, floor, bed, counter tops, between both of the adjoined rooms, between room service deliveries.

Even still, it felt good to get out of the room. Only a few reporters were outside the hotel this morning when we left after my dad called to let us know Mom was getting out of the hospital today.

We'd met them at their house instead of the hospital. Dad and I were in the kitchen putting the finishing touches on the lunch we'd made. Andra was keeping mom company in the living room. They were watching tv and having girls talk, no doubt.

They were cutting up to some topic on one of the daytime talk shows with several women on it. I'd just walked in as the channel 2 breaking report came on. Their conversation came to an immediate halt when the video of Keland, handcuffed and being placed in the back of a police cruiser flashed across the screen.

"Turn that up," I said to my mom as the anchor began, "Pro football player Keland Jeffreys along with his brother and his brother's girlfriend, beauty blogger Carmel Dobson, have been arrested. Initially on charges of breaking and entering at the planned site of Atlanta's Gastrafrique restaurant. We've just gotten word that those charges have since been bumped up to felony assault. In the commission of that alleged break in, one of the owner's mother's was brutally attacked."

"I *told 'ya sumting* was off about that *'gyul*, Kobe!" My mother jumped up pointing at the mugshot of Carmel plastered on the screen. "Bitch showing up out of nowhere. *Plottin'* the whole time!"

My dad came out of the kitchen when he heard all the commotion. His eyes went between mine and Andra's and the tv, to see what we were so focused on that had mom jumping up, clapping, and screaming at the tv. Concerned, he urged her in vain, "Darling you just got out of the hospital. Sit down before you hurt yourself!"

"Come on in here, Dear," Mom said, reaching for her husband lovingly, "They've caught the thieves from the restaurant!"

Dad walked further into the living room as the anchor continued on with the breaking news report.

"Now you all may remember celebrity food blogger Andra Bainswright, also co-owner of the Gastrafrique restaurant, was in the news earlier this week for allegedly scamming men to help fund the Gastrafrique brand. Authorities have now confirmed that the trio responsible for the break in is also responsible for the malicious rumors against Ms. Bainswright. This story is still unfolding but Channel 2 will keep you update—."

Mom and dad were joyously celebrating the news. Mom was fussing over me saying how lucky I was for dodging a bullet twice from the same revolver known as Carmel. Dad patted me on the back before gently chastising my mother for doing too much when she should be resting.

My focus was back on Andra. The report had ended minutes ago but she was still staring at the tv screen, eyes glistening with tears. I moved to her, wrapping her in my arms, knowing she was glad to be exonerated in the news, but still feeling guilty that this all happened because of her.

I pulled her chin again to face me, placing a gentle kiss on her lips. "Baby, It's over now. Don't cry. Don't blame yourself. Keland is a grown man who obviously has some mental issues to deal with."

"Yeah," my mother co-signed, going off again, "It surely isn't your fault baby girl, that jealous ass Carmel, was plotting the whole time. She was always jealous of you and your relationship with my baby. Not surprised she been plotting against ya' all these years..." her words trailed off as she finally noticed mine and Andra's embrace. "Oh, um," She sputtered, finally cocking her head to the side as a smile slowly spread on her face.

Understanding the shift that had his wife about to spill over with joy, Dad cleared his throat, breaking the awkward silence. He patted Mom lovingly on the shoulder before helping her up. "Lunch is ready, baby. Come on here and help me fix the plates while these two talk." He ushered mom into the kitchen, turning to give me a wink as he disappeared through the double doors.

"Kobe, I almost ruined everything. And your mom. God. She was hurt behind all this."

"Mom is ok. Gastrafrique is ok. We are ok." I said, comforting her. She smiled weakly at those words. "Plus, I need you to clear up those tears quickly, because there is a woman in that kitchen who is ready to burst at the seams with questions."

At that Andra giggled. "Yeah, if she didn't know that her son was screwing her fake daughter, she does now." We were both laughing at that when Andra's phone rang. "It's my dad," she said, answering. "Hey dad. Really? Ok. Kobe's right here. Putting you on speaker phone."

"I hope you two have seen the news by now," Leboo said.

We both answered yes in unison.

"Okiyo was able to get info from local authorities and access to footage from nearby CCTV cameras. They were able to pinpoint who the culprits were using facial recognition software."

"CIA nigga," Andra mouthed over the phone, twisting her lips, and raising her eyebrows at me knowingly.

Leboo continued, "Apparently this guy Keland and his brother had been casing the joint trying to ambush Kobe, believing that Andra had dissed him for you. They used Carmel to get close to you. She was the one who disarmed the alarm the first time and was supposed to disarm it on the second break in, but Kobe's mom being their foiled their plans."

"Yo," I said, hands to my head, "I knew, I'd set that alarm."

"Yes, Son. You did. And Andra, rest assured, you have been fully exonerated from all negative allegations."

I moved behind her, circling my arms around her waist as she sank into me. She dropped her head back on my shoulder as she breathed a sigh of relief. As a thought occurred, she refocused on the phone, speaking to her father, "Ok. So what does this mean for the show?"

"Ahh, baby gourd. Good news. With all this blowing over, the studio is even more excited about the show. Not only do they want to launch on schedule and as planned, the show will also be airing in the primetime slot expanded across all markets and translated in 6 languages."

"Oh my god," she yelled, turning in my arms jumping for joy, handing me the phone, bracketing my face with both hands and pressing her lips to mine." My mom and dad were in the doorway of the kitchen smiling at us and at the good news. Leboo's voice cut through the revelry. "Hold on. There's more."

"More?" I spoke over Andra's squealing. "What more can there be?"

Leboo chuckled over our excitement and continued, "The studio wants to offer a multi-year deal for the show and depending on the successful launch of the restaurant, they want to open up additional locations in Paris, Ghana and Tokyo!"

I stumbled at that last bit of news. The dream we'd had since we were kids had come true ten times over.

Epilogue – Andra (Two Years Later)

♥

I STEPPED INTO THE restaurant, my heart swelled with pride, taking in the incredible scene before me. A mix of warm colors, earthy tones, and vibrant African patterns adorned the walls, reflecting our passion for the continent's diverse cultures.

As I did every time I entered the space, I stood in awe at the feature wall Kobe had commissioned in my honor. He'd hired a local artist to do a mosaic mural depicting Maasai Warriors performing *Adumu*, the ritual jumping dance. The entire mural was created using beads, sourced directly from the women of the Maasai Mara. The very beads that I still wore around my wrist every day.

Twinkling lights cast a magical glow on the eclectic collection of African art that graced every corner, and the air was filled with an intoxicating blend of West and East African spices. The atmosphere was jubilant, with African beats playing softly in the background, making it nearly impossible not to move my hips to the rhythm.

I smiled as I saw all our hard work and love for African culture manifest in the beautiful space we had created. The restaurant was alive with celebration and joy, and I was grateful for the amazing journey Kobe and I had embarked on together. It was a testament to our dedication and dreams that we had transformed our humble food blog into this thriving restaurant, now awarded with a coveted Michelin star.

I felt Kobe's presence before I saw him. He'd been in the back getting ready for the party. Nevermind, that it was in his honor, he showed up and worked right along with his staff guiding, tasting, and reviewing each savory dish that would be served tonight.

Now, here he was invading my senses smelling good, looking dapper in his well-tailored suit. I could eat him up. Guests be damned. I would have gladly allowed him to take me in that kitchen to recreate that damn dream I'd had about him so long ago.

His eyes met mine, and he walked towards me with a warm smile, wrapping his arms around my waist, pulling me close so we could sway together to the hypnotic music of Fela Kuti, playing through the sound system. He bent down nuzzling my neck softly before whispering in my ear, "We've come a long way since our food blog days?"

I smiled up at him, intoxicated by the love and happiness that teased the corners of his eyes. "Yeah, we have. Hell, we've come a long way, period. You're no longer that scrawny little boy with a thick African accent. Though I wish you still had it," I frowned, sucking my teeth and twisting my lips at him.

"And I've finally grown into those big ass teeth I used to have back in middle school."

He threw his head back and laughed at my silliness.

"Big teeth and all, I still thought you were the most beautiful thing I'd ever seen in my life. Still do."

A surge of love gushed over me as I gazed into his eyes. Kobe's lips found mine in a passionate kiss, making my heart race and my entire body tingle with joy. I pulled back, still feeling a warmth deep in my chest.

"We did it, Kobe," I squealed, remembering the last time I'd said the same words to him the night we announced Gastrafrique making it to five million followers.

We'd almost tripled that number now and we were certified celebrities. I pecked him on the lips again before finishing, "I couldn't have asked for a better friend— partner, in love, life or business."

"Ditto, *gyul*," he smiled down at me, taking my hand so we could make our way through the room. We mingled with our guests, thanking them for coming, sharing stories of our journey with some, laughing, and catching up with others. It was surreal.

My dad flew in for the festivities accompanied by Okiyo and my sister of all people. My heart swelled to watch my father and mother chatting and laughing together. Their relationship had blossomed over time, and it warmed my heart to see them finding common ground after all these years.

Kobe's voice rose over the hum of conversation. "Everyone, please raise a glass to Gastrafrique and our amazing journey!" As our loved ones raised their glasses in a toast, the sense of accomplishment and unity was palpable.

We continued to weave through the crowd, each of us stopping to share a moment or a story with our loved ones. Aunt Vi and Uncle Tre, always the life of the party, regaled us with tales of their latest trip to Maldives.

My half-sister, Makena, and I exchanged a glance and she raised her champagne flute to us and even offered genuine congratulations. Our relationship was still a work in progress. I mean we weren't lovey, dovey or close by any stretch of the imagination, but we were both making strides to understand and accept one another.

As Kobe and I conversed with his parents, their pride was on full display. "Our son is a Michelin-starred chef!" Mrs. Abara exclaimed. "Now, if there were wedding bells a-ringing, my life would be complete," she said smiling, resting her hand on Kobe's arm.

She smacked her husband playfully when he rolled his eyes at her wedding shenanigans. "Come on here and leave these kids alone," he *tsked*. Sucking his teeth at his wife.

Kobe bashfully grinned down at me. "In due time, Mama. In due time."

His words were a promise to me, but he continued to his mother, "Tonight we celebrate this star. And I couldn't have done it without Andra by my side. She's been my rock through all of this."

Lost in his gaze, I couldn't help but wonder how a girl like me was so lucky to have this sexy man in her life.

As we continued to mingle, I was suddenly faced with a familiar figure. "Rhiyan?"

Her eyes widened in recognition, and she let out a surprised laugh. "Andra? Hey girl!" She squealed, embracing me warmly. She turned to the gorgeous hunk of a man standing off to the side behind her. "Babe, you remember the young lady I told you about meeting on my flight to Bali before I met you?"

He stepped up, reaching out a hand first to Kobe, then to me before answering his wife. "The young lady who'd moved to Kenya, right?" He said brows quirked as he looked down at his wife.

"Yes," she exclaimed excitedly. "Girl I gushed for days about the ATLien who'd moved to the motherland. Told him about Sister's

Traveling Solo and all. Oh he clowned me for days when I told him that I would tell people I was a sister traveling solo because I was embarrassed to say I was a pitiful soul going to Bali to find myself."

Her husband kissed her lovingly before grabbing her hand, comforting her when he said, "But if you hadn't, I wouldn't have found you."

The love that was in her eyes when she looked at him was everything. Then as if remembering her manners, Rhiyan smiled as she introduced her husband, Kendrick, their daughter, Jada, and Kendrick's aunt Ona before continuing, "The restaurant is stunning, Andra! And this must be the business partner you so casually mentioned on that flight?" She raised an eyebrow at Kobe this time, a grin playing at the corners of her mouth.

"Oh yes," I said, also remembering my manners, "This is Kobena Abara, known by Chef Kobe to most and the reason behind this Michelin star we are celebrating tonight. I beamed at him so proud.

Not missing a beat, Rhiyan winked at me, "Some business partner," before holding up a hand to her mouth in a faux whisper, "He's gorgeous." Kobe greeted everyone, a bashful grin ever on his face as if he didn't know how handsome he was.

We stood there chatting with Rhiyan and her family for a while longer. It was serendipitous to find out that she was the developer for Parque Place and had brought her team out to celebrate the restaurant that had won a Michelin star, having no idea that it was the very same restaurant I told her about on our chance meeting on a flight to LA.

They congratulated us on the win, Rhiyan stating, "You two have created something special here. The rich blend of African food and culture you've brought to Parque Place, to Atlanta, is simply breathtaking."

Before long, everyone was seated enjoying platters of succulent jollof rice, aromatic *doro wat*, and mouthwatering *ugali*. The mingling scents of savory and sweet dishes created an irresistible aroma that tantalized the senses.

As the evening progressed, Kobe and I split up, continuing to enjoy our guests. I saw Okiyo in my periphery and couldn't help but notice my father's head of security stealing glances at Rhiyan's assistant, Delia. I was floored to see this proper British gentleman subtly flirting with the petite beauty. *Let me find out that CIA was smitten.*

In between conversations, Kobe and I stole a quiet moment together. The party continued around us, a testament to the love and support that had carried us through the years. It was a perfect blend of joy, nostalgia, and anticipation for the future. As I gazed into Kobe's eyes, the weight of our accomplishments and his love cloaked me like the warmest *shuka* of my people.

"Andra," Kobe whispered, his hand finding mine, "thank you for being my inspiration, my partner, and my best friend."

I squeezed his hand and smiled. "Kobe, we were destined to be together. From the moment we met, I knew that we shared something unique. I can't imagine my life without you."

We stood there, fingers intertwined, as the laughter and joy of our loved ones filled the air. It could have been a perfect end to our story, and yet, it was only the beginning. A new chapter in our lives. As we looked out at the faces of the people who had supported and loved us through it all. The little girl who had once felt abandoned was loved. A lot.

The Michelin star was just another milestone in our Gastrafrique journey—and these two African Food Freaks stood hand in hand reveling in the atmosphere of the night, ready to take on the rest of what was to come for Gastrafrique. Hard work, love, and passion for African food got us here. Our love for each other would take us beyond the brand.

The End

The End

Thank you for reading "Mess on the Mara." Please consider leaving an honest review about this work on the site where you purchased or on Amazon at the QR code below.

A QR Code to submit an honest review on Amazon.

About the Author

C HER TERAIS IS THE ultimate Renaissance woman! With a passion for travel and an eye for gorgeous interior design and architecture, she's crafted beautiful stories centered around black love and its complexities.

Take a journey with her from busy street markets to distant escapes in her books that will take you around the world.

Originally from Warner Robins, Georgia, Cher spent time in the Army before moving to the Middle East as a Program Manager. Her travels allowed her to dive into diverse cultures as well as serve as a springboard for more trips around Asia, the Caribbean and Europe. Proud mother of two daughters and one grandson, Cher encourages them to pursue their dreams of no limits!

Follow her on social media (@cher_terais (all major platforms) @cher_terais_author on TikTok) to learn more about this amazing author who calls the suburbs of Atlanta home!

Don't forget to checkout other books in the **Wanderlust Romance series!**

Bali Blue

Tempest in Tulum

Stay even more connected by scanning the QR Code below to get bonus content for Cher Terais's books. Discover the fun things like:

The soundtrack to this book and the others

Inspiration boards and visuals for each book;

Free downloadables, short stories and more!

https://linktr.ee/Cher_Terais

The trip doesn't stop here! *The Booked Club* community and podcast are COMING SOON!

Sign up for my mailing list for more details!